D0621824

PRAISE FOR

FINDING SGT. KENT

"In Hutson's novel, a soldier returns home, haunted by memories of war, and tries to track down family members he's never known.

"Robert Kent served as a sniper in Afghanistan, rising to the rank of master sergeant before he was discharged after some 15 years of service. Now he finds himself in a veteran's hospital, alone and plagued by memories of past violence, emotionally lost but not yet ready to surrender to despair. Dr. Zilker, his preternaturally patient therapist, prods him to discuss the last day of his tour of duty in Afghanistan, during which he was involved in a ferocious firefight and badly wounded. Over the course of three tours, he was awarded two Purple Hearts and a Silver Star Medal, but they provide him with no relief from his nightmares. Before he enlisted, he had a difficult childhood—he never knew his Vietnam-veteran father, and his mother drank herself to death when he was 15. He was taken in by a foster family, the Dunhams, in his teens. At Zilker's encouragement, Robert decides to track down his surviving relations, aided by little more than his parents' names and letters that his father wrote to his mother while serving overseas. Hutson palpably depicts Robert's longing to get to know his family members, and, by extension, his desire to discover something new about himself: "now I was going to get to turn over all the pieces on the game board." The author's prose artfully balances a poetical sensitivity with the gritty anger of his protagonist. Also, his descriptions of military life—and of combat, in particular—feel impressively authentic. The novel's chief source of strength, however, is the author's literary restraint; it's a study in the raw power of unsentimental expression, as well as an extension of Robert's wounded laconicism. The book offers a sensitive look at the psychological ramifications of combat, raising tough questions without offering facile answers.

"A poignant dramatization of the emotional fallout of war."

—KIRKUS REVIEWS

"As a veteran of every American war from Grenada to the current War on Terror, I found Sergeant Kent's journey of self-discovery a model of self healing, applicable to all combat veterans, past and present. Valuable and entertaining reading for anyone who knows a combat vet and hopes to understand them better."

—DENNIS WOODS, CSM RETIRED, AUTHOR OF *BLACK FLAG JOURNALS*

"An intimate journey with a returning veteran who trusts no one, including himself. Hutson's empathic narrative explores the psychological ramifications of war in a single voice that rings true, captivates and endears."

—JEFFREY HESS, AUTHOR OF *BEACHHEAD, TUSHHOG*, AND *COLD WAR CANOE CLUB*

FINDING
SGT. KENT

Raymond Hutson

VIRGINIA BEACH
CAPE CHARLES

Finding Sgt. Kent
by Raymond Hutson

© Copyright 2018 Raymond Hutson

ISBN 978-1-63393-622-5

All rights reserved. No part of this publication may be reproduced, stored in a retrieval system, or transmitted in any form or by any means – electronic, mechanical, photocopy, recording, or any other – except for brief quotations in printed reviews, without the prior written permission of the author.

This is a work of fiction. The characters are fictitious. With the exception of verified historical events and persons, all incidents, descriptions, dialogue and opinions expressed are the products of the author's imagination and are not to be construed as real.

Published by

◤ köehlerbooks™

210 60th Street
Virginia Beach, VA 23451
212-574-7939
www.koehlerbooks.com

For Joseph,
my son.

1

It was quiet there, a constant rush of sterile air from the ceiling vents; too cool at night, the blankets so thin you had to ask for a few extras. Too quiet to sleep, mind like a deck of cards crackling in a shuffle of images: a cave, a barley field, a boy with goats, snarling dogs, dead people. Lots of dead people. Swollen, dismembered by a blast, rippling waves of flies.

I'd cut the deck, shuffle again. Guys I'd shot; guys I didn't but should have; guys maybe I shouldn't have killed but squeezed the trigger anyway because the decision to stop was too hard to process. Guys in my platoon, and I wondered where they were now, where they had come from, but some were dead, and I'd talk with them as if they were still alive and try to remember how and where and what decisions that day might have made it turn out differently.

Then the smell would come: rotten cabbage, old blood, sewer gas. I couldn't nail it down. Soaked into my skin, waxed solid in my sinuses, it preceded me; others could smell it but said nothing. The air from the vents was odd, chemical by comparison, like the courtyard garden at Landstuhl, chlorinated and sweet.

I'd fieldstrip an M4, clean, oil, reassemble, over and over in my head. The smell gradually turned to bore cleaner, CLP, which was a good smell, from a good time of day. It meant you'd lived and had time to clean your weapon. Then another picture would materialize, I'd sit up and suck a long breath, condition red. Eventually they found the right medication and sleep fell like a shroud.

Down the hall a guy cried most of the night until they gave him something to knock him out as well. I had a window that didn't open, a view of jack pines on hillsides five miles away, the glass woven through with a checkerboard of fine wire to keep it from breaking if you threw something at it, but the dishes were all Styrofoam, the furniture screwed to the floor, so there really wasn't anything to throw. They turned down the hall lights at 2100; the room lights turned off, but the light in the latrine clicked on with any motion in the room, even a cough, so they could always see where you were. You couldn't shut the door to the toilet because there wasn't one, so it was noisy after dinner with everybody taking a dump.

Above the sink was a mirror—not real glass but a wavy piece of polished stainless steel. Someone had scratched *FUC* across the surface, leaving plenty of room for a *K*, but maybe they'd been interrupted, or just forgot what they wanted to write. I didn't look right in that surface; nothing did, details merging in a foggy glare.

At 0600 the day-shift nurses arrived with voices like elephants, the glass doors of the nurse's station slamming with each arrival, each departure, digging in purses for car keys or cigarettes as they rambled toward the ward doors and buzzed out. A food cart rolled past. After a few minutes Barb would stick her nose in, flip the lights on, and say something trite and stupid that she thought would put me in a positive frame of mind. Barbara Susskind, R.N. Barb. Like a thorn. I called her Sunshine.

From the breakfast room you could look about ten blocks east through a residential section of low, one-story ranchers built in the Fifties, asphalt shingle roofs and big backyards, a pale-yellow house I estimated at about 200 meters. At 250 meters, a white house with roses between the sidewalk and the curb. Someone's grandmother watered them each morning about 0730, the trees moving with a southwest breeze, five to ten knots, one minute of angle. A 7.62 round would drop about four inches at that range. I had no notions of killing the woman, just a game I played with myself.

My foster dad used to take me deer hunting each fall, said I was a natural. I could almost see the course of the bullet—the fall with gravity, its gentle arc in a crosswind, a single motion born in a thought, a gentle squeeze, the flash of a primer, and everything that followed until the impact with flesh.

"What are you looking at, Mr. Kent?" Sunshine hovered by my shoulder.

"Roses. Down the block there."

"You like roses?"

It was a diagnostic question and I ignored her. She loitered a moment and moved away.

Cheerios every morning. Hard to fuck up Cheerios. Get the oatmeal and you'd have to hold the bowl down with one hand. All the coffee you wanted—but all decaf. Marsden the Mormon would have been happy there. Saw him sitting in the dark dining room when I was admitted. He saluted, a casual wave, really, and I nodded. Marsden would have been ecstatic just to be alive.

Guzman landed opposite me at the next table, flopped his fat arms on the surface, shook his Indian hair out of his face. We usually kept a wide perimeter. The ward was designed for thirty patients, but we were twelve.

"Zilker got in your head yet?" he asked.

Stony Dr. Zilker; penetrating but neutral, you couldn't stare him down. One time during the first couple of nights, he was standing in my door, motionless, silent.

"He get in yours?" I asked.

"Yeah. He said it was fuckin' scary."

Nurses talked. Guzman was there four or five times a year. If he ran out of meth or couldn't make the rent, he'd show up and say he was going to hurt himself.

"Guzman, you such a badass. How come you can't take out one parasitic junkie?"

"Who?"

"One in the mirror."

If he were for real, he would have put the hurt on me. He spotted another table and picked up his tray.

After breakfast, I'd walk the ward twenty-two times, use the toilet, throw a pillow at the base of the room door to hold it shut. I'm not modest, just feel vulnerable with pants around my ankles. I'm still getting used to the freedom of sitting on a toilet without thirty-five pounds of body armor hanging on my torso. You couldn't just take it off and lay it on the floor.

One of the latrines in Camp Eggers had a drawing on the back of the stall door of our commander in chief, grimacing, wearing body armor, full field pack, Kevlar helmet propped on those huge ears, his skinny little lawyer-ass crushed against the seat, VP trying to help him to his feet.

Keeping Zilker at bay was easy at first. I didn't talk. No talking and the process stopped, whatever he wanted anyway, like a potato in a tailpipe. "Indifferent," I'd said. It was the only word I'd given him, and I was bluntly honest. I felt indifferent about the things I'd done, and the things that had been done to me.

"You could be in jail right now," he said at the first interview.

I didn't look at him, had nothing to say.

"Machinery of the law isn't that sensitive. You just got lucky."

"You think I should be in jail, sir?"

"I think that would be a waste."

I stared at my feet.

We were on our third week of such nonsense when it became clear that the nurses were telling him that I *could* talk, that I joked with them, that I was, most of the time, *appropriate*.

A new tablet, a little blue one, eventually appeared in my morning med cup, and an hour later at the interview Zilker opened with, "Today we're going to cut the bullshit." But he didn't seem angry about it, sort of friendly and matter-of-fact, and it seemed like a pretty good idea. The whole world seemed a friendlier place for a few hours.

- - -

It was labeled *Lounge,* but wired double-glass windows separated it from the hall. The doorknob didn't lock on the inside. There were six padded armchairs of blond oak around a matching table. A sofa, one cushion stained. The nurse let me in. Zilker arrived at 1000 hours. He moved like a younger man, but the nurses said he was in his seventies. Ruddy faced, half bald, with a well-trimmed silver beard. A somber Santa Claus. He asked me to close my eyes, breathe deep, and think of something tranquil. I thought about snow and told him this. Snow falling through the pines. A hillside thick with trees, pines. Snow.

"What are your goals for today, Mr. Kent?" He always started like that.

"To convince you I'm well, sir."

"Are you sick?"

"Someone thought so, sir."

"You don't need to call me *sir.* You're discharged. Honorably, at that."

"Yes sir."

He rubbed his closed eyes like he was weary of this chase, which hadn't started yet today but would, like it had for three weeks. He was a patient sonofabitch.

"Three tours, two Purple Hearts. A Silver Star, charged the enemy in a cave in 2002, killed eight insurgents, wounded."

"I *fell* into the cave, sir. Chasing *one* guy. Other seven were a big surprise."

"Likely saved your platoon."

"We were better riflemen." It was true. Taliban shot from the hip, spray and pray. If Allah wanted you to die, their bullet would find you.

"Then an Article 93."

"It was dismissed, sir."

"I know." He sat up straighter, opened his eyes. "Which is all the more reason you should be able to talk about it. The incident that landed you here has been dismissed too. You don't have any trouble talking about that, do you?"

5

I had been waiting in the lounge of a restaurant, a nice place I'd become a regular at, to meet a girl from Match.com. No-show. I went out the back and some jerk was trying to break into a car, had himself a slim jim, just popping the lock open, and I nailed him, tied his hands to the car door, when the police roll up. It turned out the guy was getting into his *own* car, had locked the keys inside. I was in some kind of mood, so they arrested me, figured out I was a vet that wasn't quite right, and dumped me at the VA hospital. The guy turned out to be another vet and dropped charges. Zilker heard all of this, twice.

"They tased you, Robert. They don't do that just because somebody's in a bad mood. You were probably scaring them."

"Pepper sprayed me too." You get teargassed in boot camp, though, and learn to deal with it. I rubbed my chest gently, a little scab there from one of the needles. "When am I getting out of here?"

"You think you're ready to leave? You still can't talk about your last day in the field."

He had me. If I'd had a flak vest on, I could have walked away. I would have walked, if they hadn't pushed my buttons. Since I got back it feels like everybody wants to push my fucking buttons, push each other's buttons, everybody with some arrogant fucking attitude, trouble just staying out of each other's faces. Kids are the worst.

"Robert? Let's try something easier. Talk about growing up. Why'd you join the Army?"

I looked at him. Innocent enough; he just wants to know. "My mother died. Right after I turned fifteen. Didn't have anyplace else to go."

"You didn't join when you were fifteen."

"Of course not. Had a foster family through high school. The Dunhams. They didn't have any money for college for me."

"They treat you well?"

"Wasn't too bad. Mr. Dunham worked for the border patrol; didn't talk much. Taught me how to play chess. John, his son, was a jock. Three of us went up in the hills once on horses, spent the weekend, Mr. Dunham pointing out what he knew about the stars, and every tree we passed. John was bored, rolling his eyes"

"You get along with John?"

"He had to share his room with me. Resented it. Pulled my bookmarks out, put my dirty underwear back in the drawer, forgot my name when his friends came by. Treated me like somebody with a disease. Had a little sister, Kaye, about nine. Got into my suitcase a few times, but overall she was a nice kid."

"Mrs. Dunham. Was there a Mrs. Dunham?"

"Yeah." The couch in the lounge seemed so available. I stood, walked over, lay down and stretched. Zilker turned his chair and smiled. "Comfortable?"

"Yeah. Very." The cushions enveloped me. Great little blue pill—nothing could harm me on that couch.

"Good. You were going to tell me about Mrs. Dunham."

"Janice. Janice Dunham drove a Volkswagen Thing she'd painted *pink*. She was younger than Mr. Dunham, ran five miles a day, did yoga. Incredible cook." Must have been my second autumn with them. Back seat full of groceries, top down, helping her carry bags into the kitchen. I relived that afternoon, smiling to myself. Several minutes passed.

Zilker cleared his throat.

"Had a nice body in a grown up, happy kind of way. Read a lot. Novels mostly. When I started picking them up she made a point of tossing them on my bed when she was finished." I yawned. "We'd talk about them sometimes." I closed my eyes. "Symbolism. I remember once she asked me if the Judge in *Blood Meridian* was a symbol of Uncle Sam."

"What'd you tell her?"

"No, I said. I think it's pretty plain he's the devil."

"I haven't read that one."

"Total, total fucking war." I felt adolescent saying it like that, and I didn't want to talk about the book anyway. The couch didn't want me talking like that either. It felt nice not being angry; I hadn't been so un-angry in years, good things coming back. Hadn't thought of Janice in a long time.

"Once, after she'd had a couple of glasses of wine, right before I graduated and I'd already announced I was going in the

Army, she hugged me. We were in the kitchen and Mr. Dunham was out of the house somewhere." I opened my eyes. "Not the kind of hug moms give their sons. Firm, fingers down my chest as she let go. My God, I remember how she felt. The lightness of her scent."

Zilker sat up, pen drooping, pad in the other hand. "Anything else between you?"

"No. *Christ* no! She was my new mom. I just remember thinking, *Going in the Army, I'll find somebody like her someday.* Wasn't going to settle for less."

Zilker turned his watch face up, seemed surprised. "We're out of time."

"She had a little streak of gray in her hair," I added, about to describe the curl, the thickness, still on the couch, trying to remember what she smelled like.

Zilker was already at the door but turned and ran his fingers over his head. "We all do. You might, too, if you'd let it grow out. Tomorrow, we talk about *your* mom."

- - -

After lunch I sat in the TV room, wondering if there was anything I'd told Zilker I could really be sure of, and watched *Bridge on the River Kwai.* One of those flicks where bullets don't leave any marks, but I love Alec Guinness. Always imagined my father might have turned out like him if he'd lived. Guzman typically sat in the back and ad-libbed all sorts of stupidity and ruined TV for everybody, made farting sounds, talked about his dick if a girl was on camera, but that day he wasn't there. Whatever Zilker had given me started wearing off, and my knee throbbed.

I stopped at the nurse's station. A piñata hung from a paperclip over the desk. Teresa sat texting. "What's the word for today?" I wanted a hydrocodone.

She looked at me and scrolled through the little screen. Screwed up her face. "Punctilious. Know what it means?" Smug girl.

"Means picky. Like, no point in being *punctilious* about the food here."

She squinted, lips moving as she read to herself. "You are so right." The only nurse there who didn't treat me like I was crazy.

"Means I win a pain pill. What's with the piñata?"

"Gina's birthday." She nodded at one of the aides sitting in the hall checking blood pressure. "We're gonna let her break it at break time."

"Is that a pun?"

We entered a village schoolhouse, my first tour in Afghanistan. They had hung a woman of about fifty, a European, from the ceiling fan days before. She was puffy, blue, foul, glasses awkwardly on her face like someone had added them later. It's always bothered me ever since, when people's glasses are crooked. Shit had run down her leg beneath her dress and dried there. Some guys started to slide a table beneath her when Lieutenant Johnson gestured us to halt, said something didn't look right, told us to clear the building. From outside he shot the corpse a couple of times with his M4. It exploded on the third, showering the room with rotting flesh, ball bearings and screws, some buried in the wall. No candy.

"Mr. Kent?" She scanned my bracelet barcode. Tablet in a paper cup. "It's not candy."

"Huh?"

"You said, 'No candy.'"

- - -

Zilker was sitting with his yellow pad when I arrived the next morning. He motioned at the chairs, the sofa. "Pick a spot. Anywhere that feels right."

I chose the sofa but sat at one end, avoiding the stain. The medication rolled over me like surf, but still I felt edgy.

"You told me yesterday your mom died when you were fifteen."

A lot of things had happened when I was fifteen. I'd been born at fifteen. I bit my lip.

"Drank herself to death."

I'd never actually spoken those words out loud and sat momentarily soaking up the sound of my own voice. I pondered that day, until Zilker cleared his throat.

"No fucking reason. I used to think when I was small that it was my fault. Later I thought she missed my father."

He was taking notes with one hand, not looking at the page, perhaps sensing some anger in my posture. "Why don't you tell me about your house first? Go there now, room to room." I went on talking about Mom, though—the first time anybody had ever asked.

"It was probably one of the better things that could have happened," I said. "She was pretty worthless. Take something out of the cart at Safeway, something I needed for school, grab a half-rack of Rainier instead. Slip one in a koozie as we drove back to our mobile in Addy, so often it became some kind of family ceremony." She felt entitled to that reward. Life was a lottery of magical events. You had to seize an advantage, hang on, hang on, learn to work the magic.

"Robert?"

Zilker stood, tapping my shoulder with his notebook.

"Yeah?"

"You fell asleep. Xanax does that." He stooped slightly to capture my gaze. "Go on. What did she tell you about your father?"

"Not much. There were three pictures over our breakfast counter. Saint Somebody playing the organ, cherubs looking down at her through clouds. Richard Nixon in a wide mat, letter to my grandparents right next to it saying how the nation was grateful for Dad's sacrifice, and a chest-up picture of my father in his class A, looking serious, *KENT* on his pocket tag, looking off somewhere over the photographer's shoulder."

"It was a style at the time," Zilker said. "My wife has a picture of me like that somewhere."

"I don't think my dad would have done that. I liked to imagine he'd look anyone right in the eye. Anyway, Mom would say, 'You're my little soldier now, Bobby.'"

I rambled on about how he made sergeant before he disappeared, my childhood rife with imagined heroism: Dad leading a platoon out of an ambush; Dad standing in the door of a Huey firing the door gun; Dad throwing himself on a grenade to save his men. He always recovered from this, through some malfunction of the grenade, or his own physical superiority. My dad single-handedly winning a war that, eventually, we lost. I looked up and Zilker had set his pen down, staring right through me.

"Doc?"

He seemed to shudder, then, present again, picked up his pen, rubbed his eyes.

"You were there."

"Right out of med school. Base hospital near Saigon." Zilker shook off the memory. "When your mother died—tell me about that day."

"The last six months she got sick almost every Sunday, puking in the toilet with the door closed. I'd lie in bed, open the windows a little, listen to cars on 395. Not even my Walkman would drown her out. One morning I went in to pee after she was done. Splatters of blood all around the rim where it hadn't flushed away. She'd be sick the rest of the day, stumbling around, taking Tylenol, drinking more beer. Eyes would get yellow, then she'd be better for a few weeks."

"Her liver?"

"Yeah. It was autumn, a week before Halloween. I was sitting in English Comp when they called me into the office, said she'd been taken to the hospital. A neighbor had come over when she noticed the car was still there, could see her lying on the floor." I can't remember the rest of the day. "When I finally got home that night, she'd bled all over, some half-assed job of mopping it up, chairs pushed back, furniture shoved out of the way by paramedics. Neighbor drove me up to Mount Carmel to see her. She was all puffy, like her bones had dissolved, just lyin' there, eyes amber, belly big, thin and tight like a water balloon, breathing fast and shallow, stink of shit in the air. I asked the nurse why she was so yellow."

I glanced at Zilker, listening so intently, but he looked over my shoulder at someone gesturing through the window in the hall. An aide opened the door, put two bottles of Aquafina on the table.

Zilker pushed a bottle over to me. "Keep going. Your mom was jaundiced."

"Mom woke up, opened her eyes and grinned, said, 'Cause I'm the Great Pumpkin, sweetie.' She had dark blood around her teeth. She closed her eyes after that. Bag of blood on a pole next to her, a lot of other bags and tubing draped everywhere. Didn't say another fucking thing, just died the following afternoon while I was at school. I remember thinking she was old, but she was actually only thirty-six."

"The age you are now."

"Hadn't thought of that. Your point?"

"You've been through a long war and still took care of yourself." He turned a page over on his pad. "So, what happened after that? That night."

"After dark went to Mom's room, checked under the mattress, then threw everything on the bed: nail polish, eye makeup, underwear, old brassieres with holes in the elastic, wads and wads of pantyhose. Found a partial box of cartridges for a gun we didn't have anymore, and an old box of condoms in the nightstand. Tried to remember if there'd ever been a man in the house. Imagining her having sex was weird. Couldn't picture it." I paused.

"Lots of kids feel that way the first time they think of it."

"I took the box back to my own room. Considered myself very lucky."

Zilker laughed.

"Found about thirty dollars in small bills from pockets and change, another four hundred in an envelope taped to the bottom of a dresser drawer." It occurred to me that I never spent that money.

I puzzled over that until Zilker nudged my foot with his.

"None of the keys in the house fit her vanity—just a cheap metal desk. I went out to the Granada, got the tire iron. There were field fires in the valley that night; I remember smoke drifting through the trees, blood orange moon above the neighbor's trailer."

Smoke, rising silent from the valley floor. It might have been Croatia. I paused, wondering if I've mixed up some memory.

"And why do you think the vanity was so important?"

"I don't know. More money, jewelry. Secrets."

"Secrets?"

"My whole life, I never felt like she told me the whole story on anything, and then she fucking dies. Like a game show, and now I was going to get to turn over all the pieces on the game board."

"I want you to hold onto that thought, about wanting the whole story. What was in the desk?"

"Bunch of old letters. Bundle of photographs, mostly Vietnam. Her high school yearbook."

"Did you read the letters?"

"Might have opened one of them. Kissy stuff. Seemed too nosy."

"For Christ's sake. You need to read them. They're both gone now, it's permissible. Where are they?"

"Mom's old suitcase. Put everything in that. Probably still at the Dunhams."

"You need to get that case. Learn anything from the yearbook?"

"*Grizzlies '70* on the cover. I flipped through it until I found her picture: Donna Palmer. Frosted hair, frosted lipstick. Found Andrew Kent in the senior section. Until then I'd had a notion they met when Dad was at Fort Lewis. Why would she lie?"

"Good question."

"I remember thinking, *I'll ask her,* and realized immediately I wasn't going to ask her anything again. Never saw it coming. Goddamnit. Was so fucking unfair."

"The unanswered story."

"Yeah. I didn't know if anything she had ever said was actually true. She'd told me my grandparents died when I was an infant. Maybe they just disowned her. Might have been anywhere. Colville, Chewelah, maybe still in Sunnyside."

"Have you looked? Online services can do that."

"Don't have a computer." It sounded lame.

"Get one."

"I would have heard from them when I was a kid. Card, money at Christmas. Phone call twice a year. Something." I stretched out on the sofa, Zilker's cocktail catching up with me. He sat patiently.

"I put Dad's photo in the suitcase last, compared that photo to the pile of garbage on the bed. Mom, her whole life so pathetic, dying in a puddle of her own shit and blood, and my father—the fucking sword of God. Kept that picture above my bed through high school."

I opened my eyes again. Zilker was walking out. I'd fallen asleep and our time was up, my knee stiff from the immobility. I stood, unsteady, and wobbled my way to the nurse's station, begged a hydrocodone. I swallowed while she watched, then went back to my room to use the toilet. It seemed odd that the bathroom light didn't come on. A heartbeat later an arm was around my throat, lifting me off the floor.

"Hey, *culero*. How you feel now?"

Guzman.

"You fat fuck." I slammed a hammer fist for his balls but hit his thigh, my other hand on his wrist. If he were choking me right I wouldn't have been able to talk. "You're just fucking yourself."

I jumped and arched my back and we both fell. Guzman screamed and let go, then stepped on my calf trying to get away. I half-nelsoned him and was about to break his arm, but he was slippery, blood oozing through his pajamas. Hesitation. Catching his foot, he tumbled forward, chin slamming the edge of the bed hard enough to break his neck. Frank and Tony, two orderlies, ran in. One of them put Guzman down on my bed, getting blood on my blanket.

They could have put him on the floor. "Get him off my bed," I said. They could wash the floor.

"What's this shit?" Tony stood in the bathroom, peeling one of the sticky meal tray labels off the motion detector. The lights came on. He turned it on his finger tip. "It's Guzman's." He turned to me. "You're supposed to tell us before shit like this happens."

"I want another blanket." I threw the bloody one out in the hall where a crowd had gathered. They dodged, let it flop on the floor.

Guzman sobbed. Someone brought a wheelchair and rolled him away. Later I learned he'd broken a rib and cut a nice big laceration in his back falling against the crown nut on top of the toilet. Everybody stayed away from me that night. The word on the ward was that I attacked Guzman, and Guzman was locked in his room for his own protection. I wondered if I'd caught anything from his blood, hepatitis or AIDS. It would be so ironic, after all I'd been through—blood spilled, dripped, sprayed on me in a life of war—to end up dying because some junkie bled on me in a hospital. It's supposed to be safe in a hospital.

Situational awareness; I'd missed it. Maybe the drugs they gave me, like a big piece of cardboard right in front of my eyes. If the enemy was there a second ago he's probably somewhere closer now. I knew Guzman didn't like to stay in his room; should have noticed he wasn't on the ward.

- - -

The next morning, I refused the blue pill. Teresa called Zilker and came back a minute later. "He wants you to take half the pill."

Seemed reasonable. I'd get half of my situational awareness back. Should be enough to keep track of Guzman, the half human.

Zilker arrived at ten and we went into the lounge, but he left the door open. It felt good to be awake, and I sat on the table.

Zilker opened with his usual inquiry about the last day in Afghanistan.

"Why don't you just get the records?" I had asked him this a dozen times.

"I've got them from the DoD, from Landstuhl." He opened a pack of gum, offered me a stick. I shook my head. "Do you have any friends, Robert? Not in the service?"

"Everyone I've known for eighteen years has been Army, sir."

"Have you looked anybody up?"

"Wouldn't know where to start." Half a blue pill started to crawl through me.

He made a face and scribbled on a piece of paper, pushed it across the table. "Website. *Together We Served.* Start there."

"Don't have a computer, sir."

"They're a couple hundred bucks. What else do you have to spend your goddamned money on? Get one." His voice raised and a nurse in the hall glanced our way. He sighed. "Ever go back to the Durhams?"

"*Dunhams.* I drove up once, they were on vacation, nobody there. Never got around to it again afterward." I'd been dating Julia at the time, 1992, cousin of one of my platoon when I was in Kuwait City, a pathologically jealous woman. She tore up my address book, opened my mail, and I just ignored it all, too busy all the time trying to catch up on sex I'd missed, telling myself it was love. A second trip to Colville was out of the question.

"You were out for three years. Reserves. How about then?"

"Went to school. Got married. Got divorced."

He scribbled on his yellow legal pad. "You feel like your time in Iraq had a bearing on the divorce?"

"No."

"Just no? Any details you want to share?"

"I was in reserves. Reserves weekends pissed her off." I crossed my arms, leaned back in my chair.

He sized up my posture, marking his pad. "How about high school?"

"Didn't really stay in touch, sir."

"You didn't or they didn't?"

"I don't know." There really hadn't been time those first twelve weeks, you'd be so tired at lights out, then Saudi Arabia and everything hush-hush. "I got a couple letters from Kaye."

"The nine-year-old."

He had this beautiful expectation on his face, and I was going to let him down. "Must have been about twelve by then. Letters always written on notebook paper."

"And you didn't answer."

"I was in Kuwait City."

"Doing things you didn't want to tell a kid?"

"Boring stuff, actually. Checkpoint duty, searching stragglers."

I remembered a beat-up yellow Nissan. Wouldn't stop. Fifty-cal shot it to pieces. No weapons inside when we dragged out what was left of the bodies. No IDs either. They always make a big deal of it in movies, but something like it happened a couple times a week.

"I helped look after some torture victims too."

Zilker raised an eyebrow.

"People the *Iraqis* tortured. They'd hook electricity to bed springs, pour water all over."

"I get the picture."

"Didn't mean to bother you."

"You didn't." Zilker closed his pad. "We were talking about the girl."

"I was just doing what I was supposed to do. But how do you tell a kid about that? I think she wanted to picture me doing heroic shit."

"Anybody else?"

"Her father wrote to me once, right at the end of boot camp. Wisdom, advice."

"Must have been nice. What'd he say?"

"I don't remember everything. Seventeen years ago." It occurred to me that Mr. Dunham made a point of reassuring me he'd keep my trunk safely stored. "One thing. He said that I'd learn from everything that happened to me. Even painful stuff."

"You think that's true?"

"I've kept my eyes open."

"What about your own father?"

"Told you about him yesterday. MIA."

"Doesn't matter. Find out who he *was*."

"I don't know if I want to, sir."

Zilker leaned forward; I'd offered him something I didn't intend.

"It's just that I think we should let people be remembered the way history saw them. What if I find out he was a drunk too?"

"Then you'll know more about him than history does. You're both decorated vets." Zilker got up and stepped around his chair. "I have a hunch if you learn more about your father, you'll end up learning more about yourself." He looked at his watch. "Here's an assignment. Might get you out of here quicker. Tomorrow I want you to tell me all about that day in"—he stopped and looked at a note—"Kamdesh. Just that one day. Nothing before it, nothing after. Anything you can remember, and then the stuff you're not sure of."

"I got shot in the knee. You've got the records."

"The knee, the foot, forty-two pieces of shrapnel. I want to know everything after the sun came up. Everything till you landed at Landstuhl."

- - -

Zilker asked me to follow him out on the smoking deck the next morning. We stood looking over the west end of town, feeling the cool breeze blow through the chain-link. Another patient stood inside the double doors, watching us, maybe to see if I'd attack Zilker. I snarled at the guy and he backed away.

"Sorry to hear about your little confrontation." Zilker pulled up a plastic chair and shoved another toward me. "Want to tell me what happened?"

I told him, not knowing if I should say I'd felt ready to break both of Guzman's arms. I knew a way to do it and chose not to, and that should have been to my credit. "What the fuck is he doing here, sir? He never saw combat."

"Everybody has their own problems. You have some time to think about your assignment?"

I sat, gestured at his brief case. "You've got it already, don't you?"

"I've got a hospital record, mostly surgical notes, five different surgeries, and a small field note from some medic named Garcia. Sent from a smart phone."

Garcia. I remembered Garcia. "Haven't thought about Garcia in a while."

"Go on. Start anywhere."

"Nice guy. Short, jovial, glasses."

"Breakfast. That day."

I tumbled every intrusive image fragment I'd struggled with since, pictured Garcia crawling on his elbows. "There wasn't any breakfast."

"No. There wasn't."

"Shit hit everywhere at 0500. They even blew up the latrine. Killed a kid named Cummings."

"And what did you do?"

"I was the designated marksman."

"Sniper. You finished sniper school in '98."

"There wasn't much sniping or recon the last month I was there."

"That morning, what did you do?"

"Grabbed an M21, a vest of magazines. Took cover in a HESCO stack, toward the south of the base. Base wasn't really finished; still waiting for more plywood."

"Were you scared?"

"We'd been on edge a couple of days. Lot of swingin' dicks coming into the valley—we could see them up in the hills—but not armed. You could shoot anybody with a weapon, a phone or walkie-talkie, but not otherwise. So, we're racing to get dug in, knowing the shit's going to come."

"That morning, what did you feel?"

"Surprised. Relieved maybe. No more wondering. I remember my boots weren't tied. I tied my boots."

"And then?"

"I had a narrow angle of fire to the south. Shot every hostile I could see through that angle as they came."

"That's where you were the whole time?"

"After ten, twenty minutes, they figured out I was there. Started trying to mortar me out."

The details fogged over, and I wondered if I should just make something up. Zilker wouldn't know. My narrow angle of view made me vulnerable to enemy approaching from my broader flanks because I couldn't see them. RPG could come in and I wouldn't be able to hide.

"I remember taking cover under a Humvee. I think I'd started working my way toward the north end of the camp. We were taking fire from the hillsides and I spent a little while scanning, maybe nailed two of them."

This part was true. I remember thinking I wouldn't get a confirmation, and how I didn't give a shit anyway. Just didn't want to die.

Zilker and I both looked down the street for a few minutes, me looking at the roses again. He glanced at me and I didn't acknowledge it, stalled him about as long as we could both tolerate the silence.

"So, you stayed under the Humvee the whole day?"

"You know I didn't."

He looked at me with that eyebrow raised again. "Keep going."

"I moved north through the camp. Was by the barracks for a while, then the barracks caught fire. Everybody retreated to more HESCOs in the center of the camp. Both of the 249s overheated about the same time, then the 240. I remember Hendricks pouring CLP all over it, smoking like burnt tires. Whole day was a clusterfuck."

"You pulled a man to safety."

"Was going to use him for cover."

"You don't mean that. Why do you say stuff like that?" he moaned and glanced in the folder. "Kid named Mortenson. Saved his life. You did a good thing. Own it."

"Mortenson." Always had a fistful of sharpies, drawing everywhere, signage over your hooch, did a very nice mural in the shitter one time, sun setting over an ocean. "He was our artist."

"When did it stop? When did the day end for you? Nightfall?"

"It was still light. I kept moving north." I stopped again, this time because I really couldn't put enough together. I crouched behind a mud wall, an RPD on the hillside somewhere ahead of me, crunching away at the mud, working its way toward my face. Zilker stared at me, and I looked at my only civilian shoes, black Nikes. "It was still afternoon." Eventually I pointed at his bag.

"What's it say in there?"

"You really don't remember where you were at the end of the day?" He pried open the attaché beside his chair, pulled out two manila folders, opened one. "Most of this is surgical stuff from Landstuhl. And a whole bunch of rehab notes."

He turned the sheets down one by one on the deck, his foot on them to keep them from blowing away, and stopped, transfixed briefly. "A blast. Overturned your Humvee." He held the page further away and squinted. "No, that was in 2003. A little TBI likely." He peeled off several more pages. "Here it is, smartphone note. *SGT KENT CNFUSED, EXPSING SELF TO ENMY FR. WOUND RT KNEE. RT FOOT. BLEEDING, UNCOOP.* L. Garcia. Transmitted from a civilian structure north of the camp. There's a written note, and then some amendments."

Zilker pawed through the folder again, then picked up the second. "Sort of a commendation, really. 'Sgt R. Kent pursued enemy to north perimeter and took a position on the second level of a residence there but was exposed and disoriented from rocket blast that occurred, with HCLOS radio contact broken. Found at scene with severed head of insurgent in grip and would not put it down.'" He closed the folder and stared at me. "That's what I was hoping you could recall. Anything familiar there?"

"There was a struggle." Imminent failure pounded inside. I wasn't going to put it together for him. I couldn't. "Shit goes by so fast you're surprised you're alive when the dust settles. I was totally fucking deaf by then, you know."

"Don't remember the head?"

"Honestly, no sir. Nothing till Landstuhl."

Zilker opened the folder again. "There was some speculation that you had decapitated the insurgent with your knife. Your captain, a fellow named"—Zilker squinted at the report— "McMasters corrected that, said that the head was from a suicide bomber. His note cleared you of the 93, eventually."

I sighed. "I don't remember that." I got up and walked around the deck while he put away the folders. Generous of McMasters, sticking his own neck out. Must have really screwed with Garcia's mind, seeing that. We'd been friends.

"I believe you," Zilker said without looking up. "You got a place to stay?"

"Sir?"

"You're not living under a bridge or anything?"

"I rented a studio out in the valley, just before I got picked up."

"I'm going to discharge you. Probably safer for you out there than in here. Not sure we're accomplishing much." He stood. "You going to hurt yourself?"

I shook my head.

He moved so he was in front of me, locked my gaze. "Hurt anybody else?"

I shook my head again.

"I need to hear it, Robert. Tell me, *I am not going to hurt myself or anybody else.*"

"I won't hurt myself. Kill myself. Won't hurt anybody."

"You hurt somebody, it's my ass on the line as well. Understood?"

I nodded.

Zilker shook my hand, then got out his gum, offered me a piece. I folded it into my mouth.

"I'm surprised you didn't check out earlier."

"Check out?"

"You could have left at any time after seventy-two hours. You're voluntary here."

"Fuck."

"Need to read the fine print at admission, young man."

"What do I do now?"

"Get a job, a day job, where you have to show up every day."

"And my disability?"

"Volunteer if you have to. But get a job where you have to meet people."

"Been trying, sir. But some people find out you're a vet, you get that feeling."

"What feeling?"

"They're scared of me."

"Then you'll need to be an ambassador of goodwill. Cut people some slack. They haven't seen everything you have."

He handed me his card and turned back to the door. "I want to see you in four weeks. Date is on the back. You need anything before that, call me. And take your meds this time, okay?" He held the door open for me, patted me on the back as we went in.

▪ ▪ ▪

Pharmacy came by, gave me a bottle of Vistaril for sleep, an antidepressant called citalopram, and six sildenafil. I had told Zilker I couldn't get a hard-on anymore, couldn't keep my mind quiet enough to dwell on a fantasy for more than thirty seconds. He didn't say much about it, but it had registered. The antidepressants didn't make sense to me, like having gangrene of the leg and taking a pill to keep anybody from smelling it. I could hurt people if I wanted, kill them from half a mile away. I just didn't want to. If I did, a little tan pill wasn't going to make any difference.

I packed the contents of my nightstand in a plastic bag and retrieved my small Gerber from the VA police as I left. All the while, I could not deny the one little voice—the agonizing fact that rose at every pause in my thoughts; the inconsistency that Zilker hadn't recognized, or, if he had, he was waiting for me to square up with him. He'd been a doc in the Army before he came here. In Vietnam. Maybe he was thinking it as he handed me his card. I tried to remember if there was anything written on his face.

There were precious few suicide bombers outside the cities in Afghanistan. The Taliban in the field didn't prefer to work that way. There sure as hell weren't any that day in Kamdesh.

And any idiot, especially Zilker, a doctor, would know a head removed by an edged weapon looked very different from one separated by a blast.

Causality. Correlation does not imply causation. I wanted to know that *this* led to *that*, and *that* could cause something for certain. Just a Möbius loop going around in my head. *Why did the knife come out of the sheath?* Parts were out of order, parts were missing, and I didn't know how to tell anyone.

2

I rode the bus my first week there, trash on the seats and down the aisle, a rolling chamber of emptiness. In my car, or alone, it was different. But here I was, back on the bus, working through different arguments with the impound lot on why I shouldn't be penalized, not wanting to play the poor Army vet card, figuring the car had been towed. It took me a second or two to recognize my green Corolla, but it was still in the parking lot behind Doughty's, raindrop blotches of dust on the windows, a half-empty PBR can on the hood. I bought it from Dollar Rent-A-Car three days before I was picked up. There were two green ones and a maroon that day. I picked green to blend in. Cars are supposed to say who you are, and I didn't want to be anybody. Green is earth, foliage. Green is camouflage.

Terry, one of the owners, was dragging the garbage out and offered a half-hearted salute. "Looked for you in the obits, didn't see anything. Figured you'd be back." He wiped his hands on his apron and took a few steps my way.

"Was at the VA. Unexpected. Thanks for not having me towed."

"No problem." He disappeared into the kitchen.

I backed in the Toyota at the apartment, a ways from the doors but visible from my balcony, half the other vehicles parked cockeyed, angled, taking up two spots. I always picked the same spot, if some asshole hadn't taken it already. I grabbed a crushed Zips bag in the parking lot and put it in the can by the door. My mailbox was crammed with grocery ads, flyers for mobile home sales, bundles of coupons.

I flopped on the futon and threw my pack in the chair, felt beside me, then looked around the room instinctively for my M4, something I had done at least 500 times since getting out. Had to remind myself, again, I didn't have one to keep track of.

I sorted my mail. All kinds of promotional stuff: coupons, ads, shiny cardstock asking me to re-elect Kathy somebody, that she'll *really listen*, but I had nothing to say to her. A cream-colored envelope, handwritten, addressed to me. No, not handwritten, just a font that looked like it. I tore it open. The Neptune society. Had I considered cremation? Not recently, thank you. I arranged all the mail by size. Then all of the glossy stuff together, all of the dull, flat paper together. Then threw it all away.

Next door, kids squealing, thunderous TV cartoon sounds, mom yelling something unintelligible, something the kids apparently couldn't understand either because it changed nothing. It's a comfort to hear stuff like that, and I'm getting used to it.

She's had a couple of boyfriends. I've heard that too, late at night. Sometimes friendly noise, sometimes something gets broken. Doors slammed. I've seen her twice—pink tights and a butter-yellow halter. Plum lipstick. Mouse-brown hair, long bangs with a streak of purple. She didn't wear enough clothes to hide a weapon, and I could see her eyes. She didn't know how happy she'd already made me.

The second time I saw her I nodded and she smiled, a syrupy smile, and I probably re-imagined it past midnight.

- - -

It was time to get my suitcase back from the Dunhams. I'd been a goddamn fool to leave it there as long as I had, goddamn fool to let Julia bluff me, fool to expect anybody to hang onto it for so long without the courtesy of a call or letter, and I hoped they hadn't dumped it at Goodwill or lost it in a house fire. Whatever solid, tangible artifact remained of my time before the Army was preserved inside, and it seemed, instinctively, the first place to explore. The only place.

The highway to Colville was prettier than I remembered, hillsides and mountains covered in fir and jack pine, a river winding across, a train track, and farms with long, vivid pastures, lots of them, some for sale, and I wondered if that might be something I could do. Pick a place, on a hillside maybe, a view five miles across the valley, a long perimeter. And then I found myself looking at a stand of trees, or an island of basalt on the valley floor, or a collapsed barn, and I thought, *Somebody could hide there, and I'd be in their kill zone at night, and how would I stop that?* Ideas like this just creep up, stupid, paranoid thinking. And I had to admit, I didn't know a goddamn thing about farming anyway.

Maybe poppies. I marched through poppy fields all over Kandahar province. Should have taken notes, asked the locals for pointers.

A white-and-green border patrol pickup went by. Mr. Dunham could have been at the wheel. Probably not; he was close to seventy by now.

Clayton Burgers was still there. Went there once after homecoming with Michelle Williams, long satin legs, dreamy, sad eyes half-hidden under blond bangs—world's most perfect girl. We only dated twice, and I think she would have loved me like a hurricane, like she did all the stray animals she adopted; something about my being a foster kid made her want to have babies with me. Her parents were both chiropractors and lived in a big house on Loon Lake, Sunset Bay Road. I think they could tell by looking at me that something wasn't right. Maybe the alignment of my bones betrayed some illness they didn't want their daughter to catch.

I stay out of burger places now. After I'd been out of the Army a couple of days, I stopped at a Burger King in Olympia. I told the kid behind the counter, "I want a triple patty Whopper with pepper-jack on each layer, with tomato and onion on each layer. And four pieces of bacon."

He looked at me like I'd just spoken Chinese, turned around and glanced at the menu, then shrugged. I repeated myself, slower, because maybe I'd spoken too fast, and followed it with "Do you understand me?"

He shrugged again. "I dunno."

I reached across the counter and took his tiny little bicep, like I might have with any new recruit. "If it's not on the menu can you make it? I have money." I waved a twenty under his nose.

He tugged sideways, said something like "Chill, dude," or some kind of bullshit. I grabbed a fistful of his shirt and dragged him onto the counter.

"What I'd like to hear from you—" and right then I realized I was out of line, but I went on, because I had started, and it is important to follow through to maintain credibility. "I want to hear 'Yes sir.' Or 'No sir.' Or 'I don't know, but I will find out, sir.'"

Two cops walked in about that time and one wrist-locked me, the other put a baton under my jaw, and the three of us crab-walked outside. I had my Army greens on and a few battle ribbons, even though technically I was a civilian by that time. They asked me how long I'd been out, what I thought I was doing, and were entirely unsympathetic with my point of view. I could be cuffed, booked, or I could go back and apologize.

I have come to understand that such displays of aggression are considered an "anger control" problem, but I wasn't angry. I was trying to make my point heard, and if one is not understood at first, you must clarify. I was used to being listened to. What I said to the men in my platoon was important. You rag on your guys because you want them all to stay alive, don't want to write to some kid's mom that her son didn't listen and fucked up and now he's in a bunch of pieces, so please try to remember how he looked when he enlisted. But that shift in my tone—how important something is to me at the moment—can happen suddenly, I've learned. I don't know if it's way over those hilltops across the valley or just off the shoulder of this road, and I could be there by just letting go of the wheel for a few seconds. Cross the centerline, kill myself and another whole family. Crazy shit. I need to tell Zilker about this, but I never think of it when I'm there. *Never let go of the wheel. Never.*

I returned to Colville on leave fifteen years earlier, unannounced, in winter. I hadn't planned to make the trip, but I took the chance to sneak away from my brief marriage. Turned out the Dunhams weren't home. My rental car didn't have snow tires and got stuck in their driveway. A day wasted, dark too soon, bleak and empty, the whole town hung with Christmas lights glowing in the fog, many broken or burned out.

I drove past the high school, which was closed for the holidays, and decided the place had nothing for me—not really a conscious decision, just some aversion in my gut. Had a new wife and that was going to be my future.

I didn't go back, always thinking that I'd write to ask Mr. Dunham to ship my suitcase to me when I got to some permanent address. When I flew back from Germany, discharged, I realized I didn't have my address book anymore, and random parts of my memory seemed to be gone. I'm not completely blank, just every once in a while something I thought I knew goes missing from my mental library.

I crossed through Chewelah and saw the sign pointing up to the ski slopes. *49 Degrees North.* Dunhams took me skiing there, eleventh grade. A few images returned—Janice Dunham in tight, turquoise ski bibs and a white turtleneck.

Driving past Addy, I crested the hill at the mobile park, but our old trailer was gone: the pink-and-white singlewide streaked with rust, a thick smell of mildew rising from the soft places under the carpet. Past the wheat fields, below where it was flat enough to farm, there would be deer in the morning, seven or eight sometimes. Mom always said she'd shoot one if we had a bigger freezer, but our only gun was a .22 autoloader she kept under her mattress. I came home one time and the TV was gone, my Nintendo and all of the games. She said someone broke in and stole them. The pistol, too.

When I told my best friend, Brandon, on the bus the next morning he said, "Your mom's an alchy. She probably sold that stuff." I wanted to punch him, but he was my friend, and the way he said it felt true, like he was doing me a favor—like everybody saw what I was too dull to notice. You couldn't punch somebody for telling the truth.

A great big expensive-looking gooseneck trailer sat in our old spot with a lot of slide-outs. They used to not allow travel trailers there. Probably having trouble now renting all the spaces. Descending the hill, three deer were crossing the highway, nonchalant. I blew my horn and they just looked at me from the shoulder.

I drove through the center of Colville, trying to spot stuff I remembered and what had changed. The Acorn Tavern, which I never explored because I was too young. A couple of furniture stores we never visited because we were too poor. Safeway, the spot near the door where Mom always parked. Beyond the loop, they'd built a Walmart, and I cruised along the strip mall beyond. A lot of rent signs and empty windows, and then, at the end, *Jones Boy CDs and DVDs, New and Used*. A Mazda minivan was parked in front, one door caved in, a khaki- black-and-red bumper sticker, battle bar of the Gulf War. It clicked: *Raymond Jones*. I stopped and went in. He was stooped over the counter and I almost didn't recognize him. He had gained fifty pounds, at least, an eagle tattooed on one forearm, flag on the other, and hair, grayed in streaks, that reached his shoulders.

"What can I do you for?" He didn't look up.

"You have *Full Metal Jacket*?"

He continued to scratch numbers on a stack of empty cases. "DVD or VHS?"

"Don't you have it on thirty-five millimeter?"

He looked at me like he was going to spit, then, uncertainly, "Bobby? Bobby Kent! I'll be goddamned!" He stepped around the counter, embraced me like a Frenchman. "Jessie, come on out here." A pimple-faced Mexican girl, about six months along, stepped out of a back room. "This here's my buddy. Went to war with me!" He turned to me. "Glad we got out when we did. Have to be some kinda goddamn fool to end up in Afghanistan."

We hadn't really served together. We graduated, both joined the Army and went through basic, during which Raymond showed a certain talent for opening locks—a talent acquired before the service, actually—that almost landed him in the Fort Lewis prison. Instead, he wound up being a gunner on a Bradley.

The girl held out her hand. "Nice to meet you." She smiled timidly, one incisor capped in gold, and turned to Raymond. "Gotta go pick up the kids." She looked maybe nineteen. Raymond tossed her a ring of keys and a minute later she was backing the Mazda.

CDs covered an end cap, surly people with lots of attitude—white guys, black guys, girl bands, all looking so postured, so pissed off. *Why is everybody in music pissed off?* Raymond seemed inured to it.

"You got kids?"

"Hers."

"Nice store. Lots of inventory." The place felt marooned, at the end of a strip mall without any people. "Looks like you're going to have another one. Doing alright?" I walked along an aisle, separating the boxes here and there with my fingertip so they lined up better.

"It picks up at night. I do all the paperwork in the mornings." He raised a clear case and a paper sleeve. The back was blank. "Get most of my stuff from Canada, comes out of China."

"Pirated?"

"Ooow," he wrinkled his nose. "I prefer 'high-profit-margin merchandise.' Tough to stay afloat in a little town. Kids don't have any money." He leaned on the counter next to the till. "You got any kids?"

"I was married. Couple of years after Iraq. Went to college.

No kids."

"So where you been, man?"

"All over."

We talked a while longer, about guys in the unit, his bagging an elk the autumn before, how Randy Grow got arrested, then got away, and was recaptured near the Canadian border. I didn't remember Randy at all, but I nodded a lot anyway.

"Bobby Anderson. Remember him?"

I didn't.

"Went in the Navy year after us. Lives over in Republic now. Bobby had a little brother, six, seven years younger."

"Yeah?"

"Name was Kevin. Went in the Marines. Second Gulf War. Fallujah and all that shit." We were alone in the shop, but he lowered his voice anyway. "Done hung himself here, just last week." He pantomimed a noose snapped tight at the side of his head.

"Fuck," I said. "I'm so sorry."

"Lucky we got out, man. Bad juju over there."

It seemed pointless to mention I'd re-upped. Would only embarrass him. I remembered him being clever—the dude who always had the final punchline at Fort Lewis. Now he just sounded trite, shallow, like someone I didn't feel comfortable sharing personal stuff with; not because he'd abuse it, but because there wasn't any kind of connection. I was sorry for his friend, but Raymond's concern was invested in the gossip value. Probably whatever had happened to Kevin was a whole lot worse than anything we'd dealt with in Iraq in '91. Raymond was just a little vacant. Too many drugs, too long adrift in the woods.

- - -

On Walnut I slowed at the corner of Hofstadter. No familiar cars or border patrol truck in the drive, just a beat-up Alero. *The Dunhams might have moved.* I rang the bell and a moment later dogs were barking and children shouting; then, adult footsteps.

The door opened a few inches and a young woman—cutoff shorts, dishtowel in hand, clear-faced and blue-eyed, blond hair knotted back with a few strands loose—regarded me uncertainly.

"Robby?"

"Yeah?" I didn't recognize her.

"Oh my God, it's you! Robby Kent!" She opened the door wide, sprang up on her toes and hugged me. "Let me get a look at you." She scanned me up and down, then turned and motioned me into the living room. "Mom and Dad aren't here right now— be home early tomorrow." She did a little dance and cupped her face with her hands. "Oh my God, I can't believe this!"

I expected to see a room full of faces, but she was alone. "Kaye?"

"Don't tell me you don't know who I am." She smiled and wiggled her torso. "I'm not a little girl anymore." She gestured me through the kitchen and opened the back door. "Janelle! Zack! Get back in here." She turned to me. "They always go out the back when the doorbell rings."

"Why?" I wasn't sure I wanted to hear the answer.

"It's complicated."

"You got married."

She swiveled into a kitchen chair. "For a while."

A boy, about four, and a girl of about six or seven dashed through the kitchen and scurried upstairs. "Their dad?"

"Tom. Tom Lutchmyer."

He was two years behind me, sophomore with bad news all around him. I forget the details.

"Why?"

"Oh, he was sweet. Had more money than anybody, had himself one badass truck." She shook a cigarette out of a pack. "Felt so good, riding way up there with him. I was eighteen."

"What happened?"

"He's down in Airway Heights." She lit the cigarette and held the pack toward me.

I shook my head.

"Got himself fourteen years, for meth. Wasn't his, though." She stood and turned to the fridge. "Somebody else just left it in our house."

"Tough break."

"I was just going to heat up some spaghetti for the kids. You wanna stay for dinner?"

Her story sounded stale, but I wanted to catch up on history. The screens were open, lilacs outside. "Sure." She was nice to look at in a down-home kind of way.

I hadn't been around many kids—mostly beggars, cutting up, bartering, worshiping, sometimes stealing from us in every hamlet I patrolled. Sometimes they were even forward observers for the Taliban. I realized I didn't really know how to talk to them.

"Wash your hands." She corralled them to the sink, squirted a blob of hand soap for each of them. "Hey, what's this?" She massaged dirt off the little girl's arm.

"Zack poked me with a piece of wire."

"Zack?"

Zack shook his head.

"Looks to me like you were climbing on the fence again."

"Oh yeah. I think that's what it was."

Kaye patted the little arm dry and kissed it. "Not nice to tell fibs. Especially about your brother."

Zack was silent most of the meal, intermittently watching me wind my noodles and trying to do the same before he eventually quit and ate them with his hands, his mother reaching over to wipe his face. Kaye had poured them each a glass of Kool-Aid and opened a couple of Coors for us.

"You're limping. You get wounded?"

"Yeah."

"Don't want to talk about it?"

"It's not that. I just don't remember much."

"One of those LEDs?"

"IEDs. No. If it'd been an IED I wouldn't be here. Just got shot, that's all."

"That's still awful."

"Wasn't much. They fixed it pretty good in Landstuhl, but then I got a fungus infection. Fucked it all up."

Zack waved his fork like a baton. "Fugged all up!"

"Zack!" Kaye hissed.

"Sorry."

Janelle spoke up precociously. "That's okay. Mommy says that all the time."

Kaye leveled her fork. "Mommy's going to say it again in a minute. You just eat your dinner." She looked at me, counting some inner clock. Her features softened. "At least you get to collect some kind of comp, don't you? Being injured and all that."

"A little bit. I'd rather have my career back."

"With people trying to kill you?"

"I made master sergeant. Could have spent the rest of my time stateside. Been a recruiter or something, finish out twenty years."

She grew somber and laid down her fork. "You gotta know, Johnny felt so bad. For you getting injured and everything, after how they treated you when you lived here."

I must have looked clueless.

"Specially the time they pummeled you so much and locked you in the closet."

"Tell him it's okay. Part of growing up."

"But when he heard 'bout that medal, he said he just couldn't believe they'd done that to a hero."

I laughed. "Tell him if he ever does it again I'm going to be really torqued. What's he doing now?"

"He's an attorney. Lives over on Mercer Island. Works for Microsoft."

"You say hello for me, okay?"

She was squirming, glancing at the counter, the sink, looking for some minor responsibility. "I could have gone. To school, I mean. Got accepted at Central. But I had Janelle."

"Doesn't mean you're any less smart. You still collect stamps?"

"I'm surprised you remember." Her smile stumbled, fell. "I put 'em away when I got out of high school. Still have the album, though. One of these guys might pick it up someday."

She walked into the hallway. "Used to be on the bookshelf here. Dad might have moved them." She came back empty-handed. "I tried to get them from every country in Europe, every place I thought I would travel someday. Then I started on Africa."

"I saved a bunch of them when I first went to Iraq. Was going to send them to you."

"But you didn't."

"I don't know what happened. You lose touch with a lot of stuff real quick over there."

She opened more beers and we sat in the living room, on the same couch I'd slept the first night I moved in with them. Cable played some sort of cop show, something that was supposed to be real-time, but they were clearing rooms silhouetted in doorways, approaching vehicles way too casually, and I squirmed or sighed or bit my lip, and Kaye must have thought I was uncomfortable.

"You got that PTSD stuff?"

"I don't know. I've forgotten a lot of things."

"Sorry I picked this show." She raised the remote and clicked a few times. "You must have had to kill a lot of people, huh?"

"A few."

She turned to the screen and we were silent for minute, watching an eighteen-wheeler cross a frozen lake.

I hugged her shoulder and tried to joke. "If I hadn't killed 'em they might've shot me in *both* knees." Her skin was smooth, warm, tanned, her muscles toned.

She turned, took my hands in hers, twisted her lips in contemplation.

"Don't get me wrong. I mean, it was a job you had to do, right?" Looking earnest. "It makes a girl feel a little better, knowing she's with somebody that can kill a man if they need to."

The tickle of her nails on my palm felt full of sex for a moment, a force rising in my groin like I hadn't felt in years, but unearned, like I wasn't really pedaling but the wheels were turning anyway. "Now that"—I pulled my hand away and pointed at the screen—"that makes my sphincter tighten. Most dangerous job in Afghanistan."

"Driving a truck in the snow?"

"Driving a truck anywhere. Big, big target. Mines, IEDs, guys with RPGs. *Nobody* wants to drive a truck over there." We sat with the kids on the floor in front of us, briefly playing the roles of perfect children, trying to assemble some yellow plastic model. Janelle finally turned and put it in my lap. "You try." She hopped up on the couch and burrowed under my other arm. Her hair smelled dirty.

It was a plastic dog, but after turning the parts several ways, it was evident at least one large piece was absent. "Maybe your dog was in a fight," I said, leaning forward. "Has some parts missing."

Janelle slipped back on the carpet and Kaye leaned into me. "You're good with them," she said, the heat of her breath in my ear, and again it raced all over my body. The truck show ended and she ordered them upstairs. She stroked my knee. "We read about the medal in the *Statesman*. Was it for that?"

"Purple Heart? Yeah."

"Is it getting better?" She stroked my knee again and left her hand there.

"Not getting any worse."

"Hey, before I forget"—she took a coaster from the end table and scribbled with a ballpoint—"here's my number. Email too. Don't lose it. Don't wanna wait eighteen years to see you again."

I shoved the coaster in my shirt pocket, ashamed to tell her I didn't own a computer, and then remembered why I'd come. "I left a suitcase here when I went away."

"After high school? Damn." She flopped back. "I wouldn't know where to begin to look. That big Samsonite you kept under your bed?"

"That was it."

We started in John's old room, now shared by her children. A thorny layer of Legos spread everywhere, stuffed animals and crushed Doritos in the carpeting, we knelt and peered under each bed with a flashlight that kept going out. No bag. I thought I saw a dead mouse.

"If Dad had known you were coming he would have got it out."

"Didn't have your number." I stood. "You guys are unlisted."

"That was Tom's fault."

We walked room to room on the second floor until I spotted the attic pull-down. "Up there?"

At the top of the ladder, a string brushed my face in the shadows, pull-chain for a couple of bare lightbulbs. The attic was stifling from the afternoon sun, and sweat ran down my scalp, across my brow, stinging my eyes by the time I found and dragged the case back to the ladder, where Kaye watched, poised on the top step. She took one end from me and we both stepped down into the cool hallway.

She wiped my face with her hand and brushed dust away from the suitcase locks. "Some fierce letters in there."

"You *read* them?"

"I was just a little girl. All Samsonite keys are the same."

I didn't know what to say. "You put them all back?"

"Exactly how I found 'em. You were still living here then. I was so scared you'd kill me."

"I still might. Goddamnit."

She followed me downstairs, telling the two children coming out of the bathroom that she'd be right back. She touched the small of my back. "Your money's still there."

I carried the case to the car and she stood behind me in the grass. Crickets trilled in the dark and a half-moon rose over the trees on the hillside.

"I'm so sorry. I didn't think it was any big deal back then." Her apology became an embrace and she leaned into me, arms around my neck, and it felt good. I found her waist and drew her pelvis against mine.

"No big deal. Just stuff from my childhood. Some of Mom's junk." I exhaled. I predicted her next words as she loosened her hold and leaned back.

"It's awful late. You want to stay here, you're sure welcome."

My palms rested on her hips, my fingers in the belt loops of her cut-offs, and it required all discipline in the face of instinct to let go. "I shouldn't, really. Got a lot to think about." I kissed her on the forehead. I started to get in the car when an inconsistency occurred to me. "Fourteen years is a long time for meth, Kaye. Somebody got killed, didn't they?"

"There was a gun. Somebody got shot and they blamed it on Tommy."

I squeezed her hand through the open window. "Could have been you. You be careful."

"Thanks." When she leaned through the car window and kissed me full on the lips, I was already turning the key.

- - -

I drove down the street and basked a little in her interest. Even if it wasn't genuine, familiarity could make it seem so. At the roundabout Chevron I started refueling the Corolla, went inside and bought a twenty-ounce Mountain Dew. When I came out, a rusty white four-wheel-drive pickup had circled the island and stopped crosswise in front of my car.

"That's him alright," someone in the cab snarled.

Three guys got out and faced me, two heavies and a smaller man, all in their twenties, wearing dusty black welding overalls.

"You sure, Jason?"

The little guy swayed erratically, and I realized they were all drunk.

"His car, for sure." He swung a fist in an arc and I leaned back, shifting my soda to the left hand. He stumbled and one of his friends caught his arm.

One of the big guys raised an eyebrow. "He thinks you're screwing his wife." I got the feeling he didn't believe it but needed to back up his buddy nonetheless.

"He *is* screwing my wife!"

"I don't even live here." I turned to my car, but the other big guy grabbed my arm.

"We need to settle this, one way or another."

I jerked my arm free. "I don't know you guys, and I don't need this."

The little guy launched a sloppy roundhouse kick, but it came up in slow motion and I grabbed his boot with my right hand. We stood there face-to-face for a few seconds. He started to hop on the other leg.

"Leggo of my goddamn foot!"

I did, pushing up slightly as I stepped back and he fell flat on his side, head bouncing off the asphalt. A police car circled and stopped, putting on its grill lights. He seemed to recognize the three, then turned to me and asked if I'd been drinking.

"Had a beer with dinner, about three hours ago."

He glanced at my Mountain Dew. "You can go."

I started the Corolla gingerly and pulled away. I'd had three beers in three hours, and I didn't need to be in any more police reports. Kid should enlist, I thought. Go to Afghanistan where everybody in the fucking country drives a Toyota, most of them Corollas. Could spend his whole short, stupid life beating them all up.

- - -

I couldn't remember anything about John pummeling me or locking me in a closet. Funny it stayed with him for so many years. An attorney for Microsoft. Probably one of hundreds, but who would have thought? I wondered what life would have dumped on me if I'd gone to college too, but that's just a what-if game, and you always lose if you play it for more than a second or two.

Radio on low, I rolled down the window and listened to the late-night highway. Kaye could use a lot of help, there was good to be done there, and I pictured her on the seat next to me, us talking in low voices, cool breeze through the window ruffling her hair, kids asleep in the back.

I thought of staying at the house. Could even go back, to her body, her smooth skin, whatever lotion she covered herself with before she got between the sheets, and it would be one sweet night to remember. Garcia had that, every night. I probably wouldn't need medication anymore if I had that. Warm sweet woman and kids asleep in the other room.

But it would be like doing my little sister, and what would

Janice Dunham think? Twenty-nine years old and floundering in a tidal wave of dysfunction. I couldn't rescue Kaye. Maybe she thought I was the same kid that lived with them at seventeen. She didn't know who I was now. I didn't even know who I was anymore. Hubby in prison for murder, her notion of truth was all over the place, and that could hurt you in an adverse situation—"We have enough ammo, honey?" "Plenty." And you look in the can and it's empty.

Janelle and Zach would be adults by the time they saw their old man again. Sort of sad but, then again, maybe better for them in the end.

Dunham killed someone once; at least, he told me before I left about killing a man, a convict, some murderer who broke out of jail in BC, border patrol called in when they thought he'd gone over the fence above Curlew. Found the guy in an abandoned cabin after sunset, almost black inside. Dunham turned to see the guy running at him and fired his .38, three shots almost on top of each other, mid-torso.

Guy had a hand axe, but Dunham couldn't even see it. His point, he said, was this: "Learn to react as you've been trained, and you'll survive. Don't hesitate. Never ever hesitate." His training had saved his life somewhere in those black mountains behind me.

\- - -

At a Texaco north of Clayton I got out and stretched my legs, bladder full of beer and caffeine. The restroom was on the dark side of the building, adjacent to an open field fully lit by the moon. The wind picked up and whispered through the firs. When I came out I stopped and looked across the field again, at a shed, and I saw them—dark robes near the trees by the shed, watching; whispers in Pashtu carried by the coming storm. I backed away, facing the field, but they never put their heads back up.

In the car I locked the doors, took the nearly empty Mountain Dew bottle and flung it out the window at the trashcan, where it bounced off and landed on the cement, the wind rolling it into the shadows. Enough of that shit, I thought. They don't fight at night. No night vision, no stomach for the darkness. No Taliban in Stevens County. I looked at myself in the rearview.

"You are totally fucked up." The bottle of Vistaril lay in the door pocket, but having pitched the Mountain Dew I had no way of washing it down. A sticker on the side said *May cause drowsiness.*

I wasn't ready to rescue anybody.

3

Bent brass sticking out of the dust cover. How in fuck did that happen? That never happens, never fuckin' happens. Can't pull it out, forward assist won't knock it loose, mag won't drop. One by one my guys stop responding, and hajjis everywhere, a smudge out of the gray sky, mass getting bigger with dust blasted forward, mini-guns shrieking long streams of tracers. Blackhawk driving them all toward my position.

I woke up on my futon, the thin sheet soaked to my back over the vinyl upholstery, mid-morning sun flooding the kitchen table. A weed-eater growled intermittently below the balcony where I'd left the door open for air. I lay there till my heart slowed, sinking, helpless, like I'd caused the death of everybody I'd ever known. Just a fucking weed-eater.

I pushed the futon into the corner when I moved in, and sleeping on my right side I can see the patio doors in the kitchen and the front door down the hallway. I keep the door open for air and so I can hear. The futon folds out into a queen, but that's an unnecessary exercise and, unfolded, the pad is thin enough to feel the steel frame in the middle. Folded, it's still wider and cleaner than just about any surface I've slept on in the past twelve years.

It's all habit.

I thought about buying a gun, but I'd be more comfortable with a rifle, maybe a shotgun, and then I'd have to worry about it getting stolen when I'm not here, and the neighbors would be freaked if I carried it in and out of the apartment all the time. I bought a machete at Harbor Freight for four dollars, and that seemed adequate. And I still have the big Gerber I was issued.

I started some coffee, used the toilet, poured a cup and got back on my bunk, staring at the unopened suitcase. I didn't have a Samsonite key. It seemed a shame to trash the latches. I'd lived without the stuff inside for so long, I could wait a little longer. I could take it to a locksmith, keep the bag and use it, but I didn't think poppy red was the best color for me if I wanted to be taken seriously. I picked up the coaster and turned it over and over. Acorn Tavern on one side, an invitation to enter Kaye's screwed up life on the other. My God, she'd turned out pretty. Just oozed sexuality. Probably not a wise path.

Someone tapped on my door around ten—three timid taps that I almost thought were across the hall, then a few braver forceful taps. I barefooted to the door and looked through the fisheye. Girl next door.

I opened the door a foot or so. "Hello?"

"I'm Jennifer, in 209? Your neighbor." She stepped back a little bit as she said this, a physical apology of some kind.

I started to lean into the door frame, trying to put her at ease, and remembered I was still in my boxers. "I know. I've seen you. What's up?"

"I feel so dorky even asking. Can you—are you good at— fixing stuff?"

"Depends." I could fix an antenna for a SINCGARS, clear a jammed M240, replace a belt on a Humvee. I didn't think she was going to ask for any of these things.

"My boyfriend put a hole in the wall. Last night." She looked around furtively, lowered her voice. "If the landlord sees it I'll be kicked out of here for sure."

"Let me get dressed." I closed the door, thought for a minute if I even wanted to follow through. Team-think. You get in the habit of helping whoever in your platoon because you all depend on each other, and what the hell else is there to do with your time anyway? I pulled on khakis and picked up my coffee. I'd take a look at her goddamn wall.

It didn't occur to me until later that maybe her boyfriend should be coming to the rescue. When I opened the door she was still waiting, pigeon-toed, looking at the floor. I tried to seem casual, friendly, but my face felt rigid. I walked ahead and she followed.

"He still here?"

"He got mad and left. Has issues."

"Got mad at you?" I asked and loosened up. "How could anybody get mad at you?" I was flirting, and it felt good.

She reached ahead of me and unlocked her door. "He was in the Special Forces."

"Which one?"

"Jared, the dark-haired—"

"No," I said. "Which Special Forces? Which branch?"

"I don't know. I think he said the Marine Scorpions one time."

"Oh yeah. Those guys," I nodded. "They are tough dudes." I'd seen Jared. He hadn't been in anybody's army. Walked like a pimp, swinging his hips side to side.

"He was doing a kind of martial arts thing."

We stopped in her hallway and she pointed at a caved-in punch mark the size of a salad bowl at head level. Her head. None of it had fallen behind the sheetrock.

"I'm surprised you didn't hear him."

"I got in late." A brassiere lay in the doorway up the hall. "I can't do all of this," I said. "Maybe get you started."

I opened the Gerber and cut a square around the whole depressed area and pulled it out. She looked dismayed when I handed it to her. "Take that to Lowe's or someplace. Get them to match the paint. They might cut a piece of wall board to size." She looked at me in disbelief. She thought I was going to do the whole damn thing with a wave of my hand. "Get them to cut a two-by-four a couple of feet long."

She stuck her head in one of the bedrooms and returned with a child's notebook and a crayon.

"Get some wall compound, wall tape. Liquid nail."

She wrote carefully—looking at me every other second or two—this magic recipe that was going to thwart her eviction.

"Try to catch me tonight and I'll give you a hand."

Her whole apartment smelled like an unflushed toilet. Keystone Light cans overflowed the garbage. Where are her kids, I wondered as I walked back to my studio. Un-fucking believable. What's the fascination with bad boys? I bet he said he'd have to kill her if he told her what he did overseas. Helpless, wanting to believe so much bullshit. All the girls love a badass.

I'd watched Mr. Dunham repair sheetrock after John and one of his basketball buddies were cutting up and left a torso-sized pocket in the bedroom wall—even held it in place while he spread the plaster. It's peculiar what stays with you.

Back in my kitchen, I sharpened the Gerber, oiled it, and put it in my pocket.

— — —

I hooked the suitcase latches with a claw hammer and popped them loose. The inside was still arranged as I'd left it eighteen years before. A bundle of letters I never bothered to read. Loose photos, square, colors worn and faded by time: a boy leaning on an old, red Ford, hair to his collar, shading his eyes. *Richard and Vicky* written on the back in a girl's hand, my mother's maybe. I turned it over again. There wasn't a girl in the photo. There were pictures of Richard on a ski lift somewhere, as well as him and another guy in swimsuits, skinny and wet by a canal bridge.

The big framed picture of my dad. White sock tied in a knot. Untied, Mom's jewelry tumbled out. My old scout uniform and five merit badges. Getting to the meetings was always a gamble, Mom sometimes too drunk to find the ignition, and other times she'd forget to pick me up, last guy on the curb outside the congregation room at First Lutheran. Scoutmaster Fitch would drive me home. Eventually I dropped out.

Another sock, $420 rolled in a rubber band, dull gray-and-green money of the Eighties. The condoms brittle in their foil packages. A couple of model cars I'd built, an old Minolta SLR camera Mr. Dunham gave me; I used it to shoot yearbook photos but never bought a copy of the book myself. Mom's death certificate, handed to me in that deaf-numb time after she died.

A high school yearbook, red faux leather frayed from the edges, spine broken and dirty. Found Mom, frosted lips and big hair, in the sophomores. Andrew Kent was pictured in the back with a sly look, not quite a smile, leaning on a '70 Malibu at the local Chevy dealer, the salesman handing him keys.

A bundle of photographs followed, mostly black and white, hour-glassed slightly by a thick rubber band that broke when I slipped it off. Quonset huts. A guy in a Jeep. Some girls in the surf somewhere, bright and smooth like I imagined California. Helicopters in long rows. A blurry photo of a helicopter in the air, and another farther away, high above mountains, taken from a helicopter's open door, machine-gun barrel in the lower left-hand corner. My dad with a mess tray in one hand, a can of Budweiser in the other. He had a stupid floppy hat.

I took the letters to the kitchen and spread them out on the table. Only one had a stamp, *6 cents, December 19, 1970, Fort Ord*; the rest just said *Free,* without any cancellation marks. Return address was a serial number and platoon on a few, *A. Kent* on others, and a couple didn't have a return. I unfolded the pages, some margined in blue, some typed on Army letterhead, others on lined notebook paper, yellow and brittle. Some were dated, others not. Some were signed *Andy,* others just had the letter *A* scribbled at the end. I moved them around and it became evident that the earliest were mostly typed, and initialed *A.* After those, one letter hand-printed and signed *A,* then all cursive scrawl and signed *Andy.*

An envelope without any writing, no letter, just a piece of tissue paper folded around a thin photograph, a different format, longer, the glossy surface crazed. I had to put it down, then look again, unsure whether what I saw was inside the boundaries of the paper, the image so incongruent with my expectations of my father, with my own calloused sense of right, my sense of belonging in this family of ghosts. I set it down. My father stood in a jungle clearing, naked from the waist up. Asian men around him wore uniforms but no rank or patches on their arms. In his right hand he cradled an FN-FAL, a rifle never issued to American troops, a long suppressor attached to the muzzle. In his left hand, hair gripped tightly in his fingers, a human head.

I picked it up again, sat back and tried to formulate some explanation justifying what seemed to have taken place. My father found the head after they captured a village. My father tried to stop one of the men in the picture from cutting it off a prisoner but was too late. The head belonged to one of his own patrol, was cut off by the enemy, and he was taking it back to be buried with the rest of the body.

The last seemed implausible because the head looked female, though it was hard to say.

All of the excuses I made were eventually upended by the expression on his face, his faint smile—a smirk, really, the same emotion coursing through him when he accepted the keys to a new Malibu at eighteen.

"My father's son. I am my father's son." I folded the tissue over it once again, put it back in the envelope and set it aside. Must have blown Mom away. Might have been a good reason for her drinking. I sat staring at the envelope, and then pushed it as far as I could across the table.

I flattened the first letter, hand-printed in blue ballpoint.

Dear Donna,   *July 7*[th]*, 1970*

We "ship" out tomorrow 0500 from Oakland. I always figured I'd be on some troop ship, but it turns out they fly you over, feed you in flight and everything. Will be in Hawaii for about an hour, will take lots of pictures –I'm joking.

It was like some kind of answer to a prayer that we got to be together on my leave, wish I'd been able to look up and see you at commencement. But your job interview was important. Your dad is going to have to fix the Nova if you're going to be driving to Union Gap every day. If not, you can use the Ford. Just keep water in it and get some insurance, please.

I meant everything I said that Sunday night up in the Horse Hills. A year is not a long time at all, in a lifetime. A lot of good ahead of us, a lot more summer nights, a lot of autumns to come. I'd plow snow from your folks' driveway every night if it meant getting to come inside to you and your righteous hot chocolate.

Lights out. Wish I was there to say that in person.

Love,
A.

They'd had sex maybe, that night. Made some promises. Movie stuff. I reached for the photo again but stopped, and instead flattened the next letter, which had been typed.

Dear Donna,

Landed okay two days ago, billeting in camp (name inked out) east of Saigon. Like an entire little city. No pleasure girls out here, my promise to you is secure.

Rained all day the first day. Had to run two laps around the camp and then Lt. Dawson (my new co.) said, 'Fuck this,' and took us all back to the chow hall, where we field stripped and reassembled our M-16s for about three hours, rain pounding down like a herd of horses. Watched 'The Wild Bunch' in the mess hall last night, none of the Mexican guys liked the way it ended.

Beautiful sunset night before last, I went out to the perimeter with the tripod you gave me, and dad's old Leica. Sentry yelled at me, then MPs--military police drove up and pulled my film out on the ground and took my camera. They called Dawson who got me off the hook, walked me back to the barracks, said I shouldn't have a tripod, just extra weight to carry. Missed the shot, it was dark by the time I got back to my bunk.

This morning two MPs came to my barracks, took me over to see a Captain Ramos, Signal Corp. I stood at attention for about five minutes while he flipped through a folder with my name on it, then handed me my camera and told me to sit down, then asked about a hundred questions about developers, film speed, f-stops, and if I really thought German cameras were all that great. Asked me about infrared film. (Remember those shots I did of the tombstones in Granger?) (You were so freaked out). He took me in the back and they have a BIG darkroom, all B&W stuff though. Two hours later I had two Nikon Fs checked out to me and was attached to the Signal Corp.

I still have to patrol with my platoon, but only carry a .45, and two cameras. I don't think the VC will shoot a guy with a camera, at least they'll try to miss the camera. A lot less weight.

Lot of humidity here, nothing like the valley. No mosquitoes on base though, they fog just about every morning.

Wish I could be waking up with you.

Love.
A.

I wondered if he had taken the photos in the bundle, but they mostly looked like Instamatic pictures, dated in the corner by a drug store. Except some of the black-and-whites. So Dad was a photographer? At some point he must have snapped, started cutting people's heads off. I heard a lot of men changed while they were there, usually for the worse. Never heard of anybody coming back from 'Nam and saying, "Well, I'm sure glad I did *that*."

I sat and looked out the back door with the last page of that letter in my hand for ten or fifteen minutes, trying to picture it, and kept thinking about Dennis Hopper with all the cameras around his neck, bat-shit crazy in the jungle.

I flattened the third letter.

Donna,

Yes, I understand completely what you tried to say. I've already been here 6 weeks, right? So just ten and a half more months to go. I can do this if you can.

No, they don't use Polaroids here. Fast isn't important. Quality is important. Definition. Composition.

I type these because it allows me to say more, and I can do it while I'm at my desk, which makes me look like I'm working. It doesn't mean I love you any less.

I saw a guy shot yesterday. We were about 20 klicks out and we started taking fire. Corporal in my platoon almost got his arm shot off. I had no idea a rifle bullet could do so much damage. I took a picture of it but Ramos says we can't really use stuff like that. I can't stop thinking about it. Except when I think of you.

I'm okay. They don't shoot a guy with a camera, remember?

All my love,
A.

Yeah. Bullets could do that. There's a cruelty about getting hit by a bullet. Bullet doesn't think or deliberate, just tears the fuck out of you. And most people don't die right away; they're looking at a part of themselves, knowing they've had the fuck torn out of them, and a piece is gone, and they have to think about that, and the whole time every molecule of air is burning like acid. I wonder if she got it, if it made sense, just how much of a shit-storm he was walking around in.

I wanted to read *her* letters now, whatever it was she sent to him, letters he sweated on, maybe bled on, that probably ended up buried or burned in Vietnam. Letters she wrote when she was young, dreamy and demanding, and wasn't a drunk.

I spread the bundle of photographs across the table, separating the color shots from the black-and-white. Only one of the square color pictures looked like it was shot in-country: a hazy, yellowed Instamatic shot, rice in the foreground, a village a hundred yards away, a soldier kneeling in the lower right corner with a ridiculously large radio on his back, old steel helmet, radio handset to ear. The rest of the color shots looked like Hawaii, a few in Japan or Hong Kong; one had the Space Needle in the background, Mom smiling, leaning on the rail at a pier somewhere, a man's shadow approaching. And the one of the boy in front of a red car, *Richard and Vicky* penciled on the back, looked like central Washington.

The black-and-whites were harder to arrange. Dad was in some of them. I moved them around, trying to create some kind of chronology, maybe watch Dad age, but he never held a camera, and had the same cocky, carefree look in most of them, right up to the photo with the decapitation, which I had set off to the right. There were ARVN soldiers in some of them, and I tried to compare faces with the men in the head photo but found no match.

I studied the roads, tried to get a sense of direction, and eventually figured out that there were two camps—one large camp with plywood buildings, concrete bunkers, in flatland, another in the mountains somewhere: tents, sandbags, really just a firebase, with what looked like 105s in the background, camouflage net all over their barrels. I glanced at the letters; maybe the typewriter didn't make it out to the jungle camp, and handwritten was best, keeping one eye on the perimeter. The handwritten notes were shorter, to the point, crude sometimes. The last typed note was dated 1 August, 1971.

Dear Donna,

I still can't believe I'm writing to my future wife! I showed your picture, and the picture of us to most of the guys in the platoon. Dawson looked at your picture and said you're a sweet heart. I still feel bad that we didn't have the whole month, but it's my fault for not making it clear when I'd be back. You needed time with your girlfriends in Vancouver. Just like I spend all my time here with the guys. (joke).

They say the pill isn't good for you, especially if you smoke, and it might be best if you quit one or the other. Now that's an exciting idea, huh! I've got to put away that idea of a family for another six months. Hope you can wait that long. Sort of taboo to talk about wanting a kid, between guys. I think it's because nobody wants to start thinking about that because it reminds them how far away they are, from what really matters. Or leaving a kid in the world if we're dead.

Now that I've re-upped, they are going to move me, out of (name inked out) up to (name inked out) to look at film taken from planes, and extra 50.00 a month. After this tour I'm done. Am saving everything I can. I added your name to my account, but you'll need to go in and sign a card for your signature to work. My dad can tell you how. Almost 3,000 saved last year, tax free. Could go a long way towards a house.

Job with the Herald Republic sounds interesting. I will send you some shots from the Huey, but can't send bodies and stuff, big 'faux pas'—French for fucking up.

A lot of people speak French here, wish I'd taken a second semester from Mrs. Rausch. But I was so busy looking at you.

Je t'aime de tout mon Coeur.
A.

I took out the yearbook and flipped through the senior section, looking for all of the Vickys I could find, wondering what sort of girlfriends my mom had, a woman who later in life didn't seem to have any friends at all, save the checker at the Safeway. *Victoria Alicia Mendez. Vicky Bos.* The first girl looked very, very Hispanic, a cross around her neck and an expression of insecurity—possibly one of the disenfranchised migrants that came for half a year and wound up in the annual. The second girl looked like a jock, and a few pages later I found her airborne in a long jump.

Donna Palmer worked on the annual staff, though it's impossible to tell what she did. Another photo, captioned *Cool types wait for the game to start*, showed a figure I thought might be her, seated in some bleachers with a couple of other girls in miniskirts, all wearing sunglasses.

I looked for Richard from the square Instamatic shot. *Richard Nelson.* A year behind her. I flipped through the book again, and at first he wasn't in any of the photos. An out-of-focus guy leaning over a paper cutter in the yearbook staff photo looked a bit like him. The curve of the shoulder, the contour of his hair. I wondered if one of the girls in the room was Vicky.

There were many pictures of Dad, most of them in a football jersey, his shoulders all the wider. One hundred and six yards in one game. Four touchdowns. Thirty points in one game. A one-man wrecking machine. Everybody on the other team probably tried to nail him. In one photo he'd even grown a pencil moustache. I didn't think high school kids were allowed do that in 1970. I flipped again through the pages. Only kid with a moustache. Even the faculty clean-shaven. Probably a case of the small-town principal turning a blind eye where sports were concerned. Girls must have been in awe.

I picked Dad out at the homecoming dance, glued at the hip to some very willowy blond with hair down to her waist. In another, he's hugging a Hispanic cheerleader, both of them with a very knowing look in their eyes. Maybe I imagined this. Maybe I wanted Dad to be the ladies' man I wasn't. I was 145 pounds when I joined the Army; I didn't even have a girl to write to, my departure from Colville going unnoticed. When I got out of the Army, 176 pounds, and I've managed to keep it solid.

I had to take a break. I slipped on my PT shorts and hit the sidewalk, limp-running three miles east on Appleway, turning off my flinch, focusing on broken bottles and dirty diapers, flattened aluminum cans in the gutters and masses of newspapers matted over the storm drains. I settled into breathing cadenced with my stride, until the road curved back to Sprague where I slowed to a march, wiping the sweat off my wrap-arounds with my shirt. I felt vulnerable. I used to run three miles with twenty pounds on my back, mostly water and ammo, another thirty pounds of body armor, some MREs, 100 rounds for the M240, one 60 mm mortar shell. We all carried at least one. M9 on my right thigh, and of course the M4, or an M21.

I ran another mile or so, and it came easier, left knee still screaming.

A girl, twenty-something, and an older lady, maybe her mom, were jogging the other way. Not many people out at noon. I tried to keep my stride long and my back up until they passed, keep the limp minimal. She was cute. Mom wasn't bad either. After they passed I slowed to circle and stooped over, knee on fire, watched my sweat drip on the pavement, wondered if I was going to vomit. A billboard on a strip mall asked if I was thinking of giving up God's greatest gift. *A baby? Or suicide?* The verbiage wasn't clear, followed by a web address. No phone number. *I think I'll have an abortion and then kill myself. Wait a minute, I'll just run up to the internet café and punch up some help. Oh, they're closed.*

I needed to buy a fucking computer; been using the one in the office at my apartment complex, even bought some paper for it, but you had to catch the manager when he was there.

I showered when I got home, blew my nose and cleared my throat loudly, let neighbor-girl Jennifer know I was pretty crude to live with. My head was clearer when I dried off and I sat down at the table and flattened the next letter, which was hand-printed.

Donna.

> *This is really a disappointment. I worked hard for that money, put my life on the line for that money, literally. There was nothing wrong with the Nova your dad couldn't have fixed in an afternoon. The Mustang is pretty, you look good in it but WE DON'T NEED IT NOW!!!! And moving to Union Gap doesn't sound good to me. I know it's closer to work. But you and I both know you were trying to get away from your mom, and guess what??? You're still her kid. Isn't going to change anything but waste a lot of money we should be saving for a house. At least get a roommate. I worry about you a lot. Now I'm worrying about us.*
> *No typewriter here, for me anyway. Not much sleep last night. A couple of big booms at about 0200 and then all kinds of small arms fire from our side, and mortars going off all over the perimeter, shit landing on our tent from 40 yards away, (yeah a tent. TENT) then a pair of Cobras came over, mini-guns buzzing like chainsaws, every fifth round a tracer, for about forty-five minutes. 'Box' (we all have nick-names here. Mine's' Ricochet') says Charlie's probably still out there, in a tunnel somewhere. That whole area, about ten acres, looked like a freshly tilled field when the sun came up. Cool to talk about now, but I don't want to die over here. Want to come back to you and start up where we left off in July. Please don't spend anymore. If you sell the Nova put it in the bank. Love you and miss you.*

A.

He was what? Twenty? What did a new Mustang cost in '71? Maybe she bought a used one, but she must have spent almost all of his savings. I was astounded at his patience. At thirty-five

I'm pretty cynical. Divorce her ass in a heartbeat. Bad news. I thought of guys in my unit, more so when I'd just enlisted, that talked about their girls doing their best friend, or some guy at college. I realize people change their mind. But to go on and on and on, not owning up to it, just like Mom . . . I flattened the letter on the table and stood looking out over the parking lot.

Jennifer was walking to the dumpster with her trash, all the beer cans together in a recycle bin. Must have been embarrassing for her. Short shorts and high-heeled sandals made of cork, long tanned legs. She swung the bags over and they thumped in the bin. She stepped up on her toes and, like a raccoon in a garbage can, probed with one arm, then the other. She tugged a two-by-four out of the trash, inspected it, and returned to the building. I stepped back from the glass so she wouldn't see me, embarrass herself. A girl who could salvage. I'd found something else to like about her.

A couple minutes passed and she tapped at my door.

"I got everything you said. I think." She was holding the two-by like a parade staff.

"Just a second." Another welcome break. I grabbed the claw hammer and pulled the machete from under the sleeper.

"That's one big-ass sword."

"It's a machete." I glanced at her. "They cut off heads with them, in some parts of the world." I pulled it out of the sheath a few inches. "This one has a saw on one side."

She'd picked up the place some since that morning. The bra was gone. A vacuum sat in the hallway.

Wherever she'd gone, they cut her a piece of sheetrock the same size. Using the hammer's length, I estimated the distance between studs, cut a length of her two-by-four with the back of the machete, put it in the hole. It wedged almost perfectly. I cut a second one while she steadied the end on a barstool, and I slathered both ends with liquid nail, muscled them into place.

"Oh yeah," she said.

"You're going to put more of this"—I held up the liquid nail—"on those, then push the sheetrock in place. Tape the edges, cover with wall compound. You might have to spread it out pretty far."

"Can't we just finish it right now?"

"Gotta let it dry. Then the compound has to dry. Might take a couple of layers to look right. Then paint."

She thanked me as I picked up my tools. I felt like I'd let her down, something in her body language. "Takes time. Be patient." I touched her upturned nose.

At the door she rested her hand on the doorframe, fingertips over mine for a second. "Come over for dinner sometime?"

"Thanks," I said. "But I keep odd hours."

There was almost nothing in her fridge when she opened it. Living hand to mouth.

I tried to be philosophical. She was like a seed on the wind; hard to say where she'd wind up. Might get her act together, be a lady carpenter five years from now. Where somebody is right now isn't a guarantee of how life's going to go for them or the folks around them. I told myself this as I unlocked my apartment, looked at the letters on the table, Mom's picture in the annual.

4

When I awoke the next morning, Jennifer was curled up naked beneath my arm, hair in my face smelling like cigarettes and pot. I rose up on one elbow to make certain it was her—a lizard tattoo up the middle of her back, head cocked sideways like it was wondering who I was. She murmured, sat straight up on the edge of the bed and walked to my bathroom without turning around, the lizard's tail swaying side to side. The toilet flushed and she was back, lying into me, and kissed me on the cheek. A mental inventory of the previous eight hours flitted by: fleeting images of her beneath me, above me, at some points an ethereal sense of terror, all mixed up with the night.

"Got a cigarette?" she asked.

"Don't smoke. Sorry." For a moment I didn't know what city I was in, what season it was, the entire morning detached from any other part of my life. I might not know my own name. *Keep talking*.

"I know I shouldn't. Trying to quit." She settled against me, lips against my neck, finger tracing my collarbone. "You had an owie there."

"Bullet," I whispered. "Matching one on the back." Garcia

wanted to stick a dart in my chest, worried my lung was going to collapse. "Went in just above the lung." I still remember Garcia pressing gauze into my chest, fist like a drill.

Her fingers crept over my trapezius and paused at the dimple there. I let my hand fall to her hip, my fingers over her buttocks.

"I'm a little foggy," I said. "I take medicine at night. Supposed to keep the nightmares away, but I black out with it too." It was a lie—I hadn't taken it for a week.

"You don't remember me coming here?"

"Was I pushy?"

"Maybe I was pushy. But you can be wild." She drew her finger down the center of my chest. "Scary as hell."

"Did I scare you?"

"You scared the piss out of those guys."

"Guys."

"Jesus. You really don't remember, do you?" She pushed the pillow against the wall and sat against it, her breasts free momentarily before she drew the sheet up, tucking it along her legs. "There were these guys, really just one guy, and I know, I know, my mistake, I fucked up." She fluttered her hands. "Just one guy. After work. He said, 'Why don't we go smoke a joint?' And it had been a bad shift."

"Shift. Where?"

"Bad Daddies. Restaurant. Really, it's just a bar. On Sprague. So we sit in his car and smoke the joint, and listen to his CD, some kind of devil-screaming shit, and he starts coming on, and I told him his music was giving me a headache." She paused. "I think I told him that, anyway. And I got out. Got in my own car."

She jumped out of bed and ran to the patio door, then strolled back to me.

"Just wanted to make sure it was still out there." She slipped under the covers and it was warm again. "When I got here, he's right behind me, and he's got another dude in the car with him, and they both got out and started to push me." She looked at me like I might know the answer. "And I'm asking myself, where'd *he* come from?"

"And I came out."

"You did."

"You're jerking my chain."

"You came out on the balcony. With a flashlight." She glanced at the kitchen table. "That one probably."

A tactical light, meant for a rifle. Bright as an arc welder. "I scared them with a flashlight?"

"You yelled, 'I'll blow your fucking heads off!' and I don't think they could see you. Stoned and everything."

"I'm really flattered. That you're here, I mean." I buried my face in my hands, tried to put a memory together. "And they just drove off, just like that?"

"Yeah. No, you said something else first. Like Indian or something. *Wassee Wah-wah?*"

I straightened up, opened my eyes. *"Tass leem shah. Wassss-lah wahchah-wah."*

"That." She pointed at me. "That scared the shit out of them. Like it was a curse or something."

The vaguest images came to mind, like the fading outline you see after staring at a bright object too long, and things could have gone very differently.

"It's from the Army. Pashtu. Means, 'Surrender, drop your weapons.'" I mustered a smile. "Had to memorize phrases. Just said it out of habit, I guess."

Her eyes narrowed, trying to measure my mood. "And I just came up, knocked to, like, thank you. You didn't have your shirt on, and it felt so good when you put your arms around me. It was all Mother Nature after that." She nodded against my head and gave me a kiss. "You really had to learn stuff like that? Bet you had to kill a whole bunch of people in the Army, didn't you?"

"A few."

"I don't know if I like that." Her voice trailed off, like she was starting to fall asleep again.

"Part of the job. Did I say anything else?"

"Not much. You were like a man possessed. Like you were gentle and everything, but we just had one thing on our minds." She tweaked my nose and kissed me again.

"We fucked."

"For about two hours. I don't think you fell asleep until about five, and then you snored. Really loud."

"Sorry."

"You didn't say much, but every once in a while you'd hold me still, like really hard, hush me with your fingers over my mouth, like you'd heard something. Then we'd go at it again."

I might have been hallucinating. Dreams get all tangled up with daylight and reality, and I thought it was getting better. I buried my nails in the pillow until they hurt. If I'd mistaken her for a threat I could have broken her neck.

"Can I see your gun?" She stood slowly and wandered naked, dazed, back to the table and, realizing the curtains were open, drew them.

"Don't have one."

"Not even a pistol? You mean you just—"

"Just a flashlight. I could have chased 'em with the machete if you liked." We laughed. "Jesus. Don't smoke pot with people you don't know. Didn't anybody ever—I mean, shit happens. Look at us."

"I don't believe in guns, anyway. And I'm not complaining." She picked up her blouse and started to pull it on, staggered, and caught herself, still naked from the waist down. "I've had my tubes tied, if you're worried about that."

When I was a child I used to think that if I didn't look at someone I'd be invisible. I pulled on my BDUs and a T-shirt like that, not looking her in the eye, embarrassed, frustrated by a loss of control apparently only I was concerned about. When I stole another glance at her she was dressed, wandering around my apartment like a stray cat, eventually bending over by my bookcase.

"Sure read a lot for an Army guy." She did a little double take. "You have a book of Man Ray." She glanced back at me. "He was one of my favorites." She pulled it out with her fingertip, leafed through a few pages in disbelief, then put it back in place. She stepped sideways, drawing her fingers over the rest of the case, mostly military field manuals, a couple of paperbacks by Bernard Lewis, Thomas Friedman. "You into surrealism?"

"No. Just liked the cover, I guess." I found the book at a Goodwill.

"I was an art major a couple of years," she exhaled wistfully. "At Eastern."

"Didn't finish?"

"Shit happens. Like you said."

She had washed off her makeup, and I was surprised how much younger she looked. She wasn't even thirty yet.

I walked her back to her door and stepped in for a minute after she unlocked it, leaving the door open. She seemed satisfied nobody had gotten in.

"Where are the kids?"

"At their dad's. Brenna and Casey."

Brenna and Casey, Brenna and Casey. Brenna and Casey. I tried to remember.

"They'll be back tonight." She looked in the empty fridge, back turned to me. "Can I make you any breakfast?"

"I've got a couple of things to get done today. I'm already late." I don't think she really wanted me to stay right then anyway.

When I got back to my apartment I showered hot, left the fan off so it would get thick with steam. I keep my hair short; only way I know it's clean. Never felt really clean in Afghanistan. Six years and always some layer of grit or oil or some little skin-eating mites burrowing in; sometimes you even had to put the same shit-stinking uniform back on.

I shampooed twice, dragging my nails across my scalp. The wash cloth had two long, irregular blue-black smudges. Jennifer's eye makeup. I pressed it deep into my face, around my neck, across my lips. I thought of Alexandra.

- - -

When I left the Army the first time in 1993, I joined the reserves, went to school a couple of years in Missoula, got an associate's in business, and married Julia, a cousin of a guy I'd known in Iraq. I couldn't find full-time work right away, did simple taxes during tax season, and ended up living in her parents' basement. I helped out on their ranch and could do anything they needed, but at some point the details of my mom came up—being candid seemed the most honest path—and they got the notion I was some kind of trailer trash. Everything I contributed after that met was with a little smirk and a nudge. I tried to give them advice here and there on how to avoid a tax or make good on an investment and her old man would grin and let me know he had a buddy that took care of the big money, thank you. Let me know they weren't looking for grandchildren too soon. I even stacked twelve tons of hay bales for them one afternoon, and they complained I left too much air and took too long. They were complacent when Julia started screwing around with the son of a rancher, and I knew then it was time for me to go. And she'd been the crazy jealous one.

Needing a purpose and still in the reserves, I requested active duty and they sent me to Kosovo in early '96, attached for a while to a UN battalion where our job was, apparently, to prevent genocide, if we happened to run across any. We started thinking of ourselves as meals-on-wheels. We went everywhere with our guns unloaded.

We were using spotlights, moving refugees into a camp north of Sarajevo one night, mostly Muslim women, when it became obvious that snipers were using the illumination to gun them down. Nobody turned the fucking lights off; it was like hunting at a feed lot. The absurdity amplified tenfold while we supervised the exhumation of a mass grave near Srebrenica. Buried for about six months, mostly boys, it seemed. Dark flesh that sloughed off the narrow pelvic bones, little bitty delicate femurs and forearms tumbling from the sleeves of blue uniforms, gold patch on the breast pocket. School blazers. Sometimes a bullet hole through the little patch, used as a target. The stench nauseated us all; not because we had not seen death—we had marched in its aftermath for two months—but because simple immersion in that odor, at that concentration, does something primal to your appetite. Obviously a bunch of kids went off to their private school one day the previous fall and never came home. UN marked it as a *military* gravesite. I fucking boiled when I understood that, asked myself what my dad would have done, like he was Jesus. Couldn't sleep, felt so phony being in uniform in front of those people, and I began to understand their indifference.

Eventually I pressured my CO to let me tag along with a Marine Corps unit actually possessing live ammunition, thinking that somebody needed to be killed for what I'd seen, and if anybody was going to kill anybody, they would be the ones to do it. After a couple of days of eating their food I explained my logic to one of their lieutenants and they choppered me back to a US Army unit that promptly flew me back to Landstuhl for a medical exam and a thirty-day medical leave. They farmed me out to a German psychiatric clinic that put me in some kind of group recreation class. I checked in and worked on jigsaw puzzles for one afternoon, and never went back. Caught a Eurorail back to Kosovo. Volunteered at a Red Cross station for the rest of that time, evenings spent drinking too much rakia, belching the sweet plum stink of it through the night.

One morning I awoke with Alexandra on my arm, sleeping in her grimy, cold eight-by-ten room, hot plate on a crate, sink in the hall, a toilet one floor below. She understood some English but couldn't read or write it, and she couldn't, or wouldn't, speak. She'd do everything to keep me from leaving at night— tug at my clothes, hang on my neck with both arms, cry. But then the sex would turn bland and passive. She clearly didn't want to be alone. She was older than me, or had aged faster, her angular, sculpted Slavic face furrowed in perpetual alarm, wide eyes, cigarette burns on her breasts, deep scars on her buttocks from the inside of her thigh to her groin. I think she had been raped with a spiked object at one time. There was a numbness about her I couldn't awaken.

In a satchel near her bed she kept a dog-eared picture of a bright-eyed boy, twelve or fourteen. She never showed it to me, but I found it the first morning I was there while she was downstairs. I got the notion it was her son. We walked the streets in the mornings and I would buy some food, and she seemed happy, sometimes radiant. We kept a mental roster of which cars were new, parked along our route to the square. When there was one you didn't recognize, it might blow up later, so you'd scurry by on the far side of the street. People at home have no idea what a blast like that is like. You don't really see it happen; it doesn't progress through stages. One minute the world is bright and normal and the next second you're hit with this wall of pressure, like a thousand nails through your body, like every bone is broken and your eardrums burst. Then dust so thick you can't see your fingers, and people who are still alive knock you down or step on you because they can't see either, and nobody can breathe. After a couple of minutes light comes down from the sky and, as the dust blows on, you see the ground and pieces of people—heads, arms, chunks of torso. They don't bleed very much because so much dust has been driven into them, through them. That happened to us once; the car was easily a block away, parked too far from the curb, like someone had just stopped in the street and walked away. I was on top of Alexandra when it cleared. I don't think she could hear me again until that night.

All of that time, three weeks or so, I convinced myself that I could actually do her some good; I stopped drinking and gave her money, food, blankets. In the end I went back to Tuzla, and when we marched through Vogosca two months later, the building we'd slept in had been demolished. I never learned if she was Croatian or Serbian.

I hadn't thought about her in ten years, but waking up with Jennifer dug it all up again, how useless I'd turned out to be when someone was counting on me. I only intervened last night because I was sleepwalking, flashing back to Nangarhar or some other shithole. I wiped the steam off the mirror and smiled, but I couldn't look sincere. The face in the mirror was ugly, damaged, not one I knew. It had seen stuff I didn't want to remember.

I threw a few changes of clothes in my backpack and got dressed, trying to look as civilian as possible. Gerber. Sunglasses. Flashlight. Might have to scare bad guys again. I flattened the letters and put them in chronologic order, leaving the last few unread in their envelopes. Medication. I took one pill out, rolled it in my palm. Puts you in condition white—not a good way to be on the highway. I dropped it back in the bottle and shoved it in a side pocket. By the time I reached I-90, I'd decided on the Yakima Valley and headed west.

I had a couple thousand bucks in my pocket to throw at this little adventure, more if I wanted to use credit cards. I get just shy of $3,600 a month in disability, tax free, with a nice lump sum three months ago. Plus about $1,500 retirement. At times it doesn't seem like a bad trade for a few nightmares and a limp. Lots of people have bad dreams and don't get paid a cent. And I could do other things and no one would keep track. Work off the books, so to speak.

I picked up a laptop at Wal-Mart on the way out of town. Sixteen-inch screen was the smallest I could find. Rest of them looked like televisions, all sorts of features for playing games, mostly war games—exaggerated perspectives of tanks, soldiers muscled like superheroes just about crawling off the boxes, sleeves rolled up, wearing some senseless mish-mash of uniforms. Two pasty kids about nineteen stood in line ahead of me debating which edition of Tour of Duty they wanted. I wanted to take them by their flabby biceps and introduce them to the recruiter I'd known eighteen years ago. Maybe introduce them to Marsden's.

- - -

A headwind came out of the southwest, fighting the Corolla all the way. An ANA soldier explained one time how Allah controls the weather, the sun, the wind. Allah sent Katrina to punish the sinful Americans living in New Orleans—everyone in Afghanistan understood that.

"Then why are you guys fighting on the same side with us?" I asked.

"Because you are repentant," he said. "The evil people were killed."

The reflectors on the side of the road bent toward me in the sun, the little 1.8 liter Toyota engine whining. Did God, Allah, want me to go the other way, or just fuck with my gas mileage?

I set the cruise control and scanned through the radio. So much attitude and none of it authentic. Maybe they should make music for people like me. Indifferent music. All the stations sounded the same, except country, but I haven't had patience for that kind of self-pity since I first heard it on Mom's table radio. Or the gooey sentimental shit with Mom and Dad and Grandpa and everybody around the fireside eating pie and grinning and playing with the baby. Nobody I ever met had a life like that.

I turned the radio off. They just keep inventing bands and idols to sell more of the same stuff, reinventing ways to capitalize on the same old juvenile angst. I never had an MP3 player like a lot of the younger guys. I liked some classical but didn't know enough about it to know what to buy. Same with jazz. In Jalalabad I'd listen to local music at night on a small Grundig with a single earpiece I bought at a PX in Germany. Monotonous, hypnotic, lyrics unintelligible, no hint of the emotion, beyond some sorrow; it was soothing and I could fall asleep to it. BBC could be heard any night, always a gentle anti-American spin. Kabul Rock was an odd mix of hip hop, Eighties, badly re-done rock and roll, sometimes in French, other times in Pashtu. The Taliban would blow up their stations every month or so, kill the engineer and the deejay, but a few weeks later they'd be back on the air. A different announcer, some guy probably nineteen or twenty thinking, *They won't get me*; that inexhaustible notion of immortality that lets everybody get up every day.

When I wasn't listening to the radio I was reading. I started with the commandant's reading list because it was implied that one could advance rank a little quicker. Then I read the same list the Marines posted, then any book I could find that had any kind of award on the cover, thinking it helped my vocabulary. After you make E-5, it dawns on you one day that you're eight or ten years older than the new guys and, if you answer them with the same kind of trash they speak, they're not confident you know anything more than they do. Discipline crumbles and somebody gets their ass shot.

I passed the exits to Ritzville. We played them once, or I should say my foster brother did, and I went along for the ride with the rest of the Dunham family, sitting next to Kaye in the back seat. There were half a dozen other little towns out across the wheat fields I wouldn't know how to get to now, wouldn't recognize if I did.

Games were always at night. Kaye would fall asleep across my lap on the way home and I'd think nothing of it. Maybe I could help her now, it occurred to me again and, almost as quick, picturing her head in my lap, I halted a selfish little fantasy. Or was that how life was supposed to work? People found somebody that satisfied their fantasies and hoped the whole business was reciprocal. It seemed very risky, that kind of negotiation.

On my second tour we had a guy in my platoon, Scott. From Idaho, I think. Scott had a rubber sex toy the size of a Coke can he'd named Gina, something he bought in a sex shop on leave somewhere, and was very protective of her. He must have hooked up with Gina almost every night, and Gina wasn't exactly quiet, made a sucking sound that the other guys started imitating. Guys would be having chow, Scott would sit down, and pretty soon somebody would start making that little noise with their mouth. Quiet night watch, and somewhere in the dark, the Gina noise. They did it well enough that once I even thought Scott was neglecting his post.

Everybody had to jerk off sometimes, everybody had porn available, it was just that everybody wasn't so *noisy*, and there was probably some jealousy as well. Mortenson offered to draw a face and breasts on her; I'm sure he would have done a good job, but it just pissed Scott off even more. He was kind of a loner, sort of autistic.

Scott kept Gina in his pack somewhere. Guys tried to steal her, and Scott would move her around. One night he couldn't find her and went hooch to hooch until she turned up, the victim, it seemed, of some kind of torture and gang-bang. He didn't say anything, just walked off, but returned with a loaded M4 and things were very tense for a few minutes. Gina was full of sand and all kinds of contamination—I think somebody poured catsup on her. She disappeared after that. I don't think Scott wanted her anymore, knowing what happened. Buried her maybe.

Lieutenant gave us a little lecture the next morning on respecting what the next guy had in his pack, and still there was a lot of snickering going on. Has always troubled me since, that someone could think of something plastic like it was a real person. Now I wondered if it was worse to have a real person and start thinking of them as something plastic.

"Find a nice girl, fuck and make babies." Must have heard Garcia say that a hundred times the last two tours. "No bigger joy than that."

When he joined us it was easy to think of him as a kid, a cherry, but he was almost my age, turned out he'd been in for five years, and the first guy I could talk to about deeper questions late in the evening. He wasn't stupid, just had a way of reducing the most complex questions to basic answers, explaining an injury or why the guys should drink their water or what was wrong with some little Afghan kid with a rash. Sat and drew a picture for a woman one time of her daughter's broken arm, how long it had to be splinted. Knew more Pashtu than me, and a lot of medical terms. Showed me his kids' pictures. Showed me a picture of his sister in Arizona, or maybe it was Texas, a nurse in an ER, said he was going to set me up with her. "Find a nice girl, Kent," and he'd slap me on the shoulder. Julia hadn't been a nice girl and hadn't wanted to make babies. Not with me anyway.

Army always made me feel like life shouldn't start yet, and whatever the last thing that I did was, I'd be remembered for that, and I didn't want to be remembered as an asshole. A few girls came and went—up-front girls, fun girls, girls who maybe were thinking the same thing. Going off and dying with an unborn kid at home wasn't going to be my legacy.

There was a girl at Fort Lewis between my first and second tours, we were both E-5s, and we used to get together in my room. We had bunk beds there; my roomie was always gone doing some Tacoma chick. Debbie would show up about every third night, we'd have some kind of charade, eventually trash that lower bunk. Afterwards just lie there an hour or so, talking. She was with logistics and the Army moved her to McAlester after six weeks, and I wrote her once, on a camp computer. She wrote back that she'd had a great time, but "all debts and friendships were canceled" when you deployed somewhere else. Followed by, "You know we're not the only ones to read these." Every time I see bunk beds I think of her.

- - -

I topped up the tank in Othello, watching low-riders and pickups rumble past, everything tossing up a little tail of dust, the trees bending in some sirocco wind coming up from the south. Tejano music was scratching away where I paid at the window, bought a bottle of Coke, familiar rancid smells in the air as I turned away. Hand on the door of my car, an Afghani proverb came to mind: *The tree does not bend unless there is wind.* An elder conveyed it through an interpreter once, and I stared at the old man, asked the interpreter what he meant.

The interpreter shrugged. "I think it means to have a safe journey, or something like that."

The old man raised his hand in a thumbs-up. Twenty minutes later we drove into an ambush. I've wondered about that phrase ever since, but still can't decipher a metaphor for danger. Some days it goes around and around in my head. A few months later a corporal told me the thumbs-up meant "fuck you" in Afghanistan.

- - -

I headed south, fewer and fewer cars coming the opposite direction, up a long, steady grade and onto a plateau, alone with the desert, into a furnace, sweat in my palms, on the wheel, beneath my legs on the seat. Far out in the sand a dirt devil danced briefly before dissolving. The afternoon sun merged with my own uneven thoughts of shadow and glare, watching for movement in the swaying fields of sagebrush, movement on the ridgeline, the uneven contour, the smudge of color or darkness that didn't belong, steel-blue shimmers of heat glistening on the horizon.

I was the point vehicle. Somewhere along that stretch I started watching the roadside for any place that might have been freshly dug, footsteps in the dust, whipping the car gently from one side to the other as irregular patches loomed out of the asphalt. Our Hummer could take a hit or two, and three of my Joes fell asleep in the heat, cherries snoozing like they were in the back of their parents' van on a family outing. Guy named Dacovitch in the front, Hendricks behind me, Marsden behind Dacovitch, squinting at the desert, said he couldn't see as well with his sunglasses on.

I hit a hole deep enough to slam the car on its springs and shouted "fuck!" A half mile blew past the car, fence flashing by; nothing rattled or shook.

"I am in Washington," I said over the wind, fingers clamped on the wheel. "I am in Washington."

I rolled the window up and turned on the air. I don't like to drive with the window up because I can't hear outside, shots or whatever. I rolled the window down. Then I rolled it most of the way up and turned on the radio. "*My baby don't mess around 'cause she loves me so and this . . .*" jack-hammered into my head. I turned it off and pulled over, killed the engine and got out.

"I am in Washington State." I walked around the car. "Hanford is over there. It is federal. No bad guys. Not here." I stood in the heat until my breathing slowed. "Federal," I repeated. "Washington State."

A spot appeared in the road on the southern horizon. It wasn't real, but it was getting bigger. Then it was real, I could hear it, a shriek I felt on the back of my neck that softened my knees. I dropped down in the culvert, elbows in the sand. A second later it shot past, an old Suburban full of Afghans. Iraqis. No, just brown faces. Mexicans probably. I watched as their brake lights flickered, then went out and they were gone, receding to the north. Had I been armed I think in that last fraction of a second as they approached I would have opened up on them. How crazy would that have been?

I urgently needed to piss, and stood below the roadside emptying my bladder, ground crackling with the wet, and a few feet from the impact a row of white ribs bulged from the sand, bleached vertebrae, a crushed skull.

"When things go down, shoot brown," guys used to say. Garcia always took exception to that.

I tried to smile, opened the trunk, unzipped the duffle and tapped out a citalopram. Should have taken it that morning. Washed it down with warm Coke. Mountains in the distance, cirrus clouds hung high in the afternoon heat, converging motionless in the south, and at that moment I might have been in any desolate, arid place in the world.

I started driving again, windows open, startled out of that spell only when the rusty orange Vernita Bridge materialized, a dull ribbon of river below it. Not another vehicle passed in either direction. Should have gone down through the Tri-Cities, stayed close to people. The little books you get at the end of a deployment advise you to tell your story, especially the bad stuff, to people you know. Really tell, over and over, to people who will really listen. This is supposed to get it out of your head. This is where Zilker starts his sessions.

I imagined Jennifer sitting on the seat next to me; I even cleared it off, tossed the Coke bottle in the back, and talked to her.

"We were on our way to a combat outpost near—" And I have to think. "It was in the Bagrami district. We were relieving the guys already there."

"Relieve?" She's smiling, doesn't understand.

"Like a shift change, except your shift lasts four months and there's no running water."

She wrinkles her nose.

"It's part of the Jalalabad highway, but it isn't really a highway. Just gravel. Really easy to bury IEDs. I'm in the second vehicle, Humvee, sitting behind the driver, when a blast goes off in front of us, a thump you feel in your chest, lifts our vehicle and drops it half sideways, pops our ears, and when the dust clears the Hummer ahead of us is upside down and burning. Whole column stops."

She just nods.

"I knew guys in there. Driver was another sergeant, black guy named Percy. Had his pelvis fractured. All this time there's fire coming in from our left. We'd driven into an L-shaped ambush." She'll want an explanation. "Something pops up in front of you, IED or RPG, or just some machinegun fire, anything to stop you. That's the short part of the L. Bunch of guys pop out of trenches they've dug, or out of the rocks, next to you, that's the long part."

"And if they pop up on both sides?"

"Then you're really fucked."

Big power lines crossed the highway, just like that day in Bagrami. It's good to remember this stuff, I think, but that was three years ago, not here.

She's understanding this now.

"My driver, guy named Chapman, gets shot through the mouth. Fortunately, he's yelling something when it happens, and the bullet goes right through one cheek and out the other, nails a tooth maybe, but he's bleeding like stink. I drag him down into the culvert closest to the fire and he has to keep his face in the dirt, mouth keeps filling up with blood." Should I tell her more? "A piece of his cheek is gone, he reaches up and feels it, puts his finger in his mouth from the side, he's panicking, and I tell him, 'It's okay, okay? Gonna have a bitchin' scar, man. Chicks will love it.' And all the time I'm trying to get a roll of gauze to stay against his face."

I found myself scanning the pavement again, had to tell myself that was then, and this is now. Washington State.

"Other guys have better cover, got out of the other side and are on the far side of the road. We engage for about fifteen or twenty minutes, then they hear the thump of Apaches coming and disappear. We found three bodies, Apaches nailed a few more."

"Not much of a battle," she says.

She doesn't understand. "Wilson, guy in forward seat next to Percy, got both his legs blown off at the hip."

"He live?"

"Only in the fucking movies. He was deader than shit when we pulled him out, intestines sticking out below his vest. Big, big fucking battle for him."

I was getting mad, and I shouldn't have gotten mad at her. She didn't believe in guns, I reminded myself. Her seat was empty; shouldn't have raised my voice. I relaxed and made her come back.

"We had a truckload of food in the back of the column, seeds, fertilizer, stuff to trade to locals for goodwill. That got blown up by a secondary IED. Guys driving the truck had to be airlifted. Taliban won that day and fucked a lot of Afghans out of stuff they needed."

"I understand," she says.

But she doesn't.

A white highway patrol car passed me going north, weaving through the islands of rock, disappearing in my rearview mirror, and it was a good ending to a bad dream. A while later I descended into the valley.

- - -

I started at the high school, remodeled and sleek as a corporate campus, but only a handful of the staff were older than myself, and only by a few years at that. No one was going to remember Andrew Kent. The librarian finally sat me in a cubicle in the reserve section of the library and stacked a pile of annuals in front of me.

"You might find *something* . . ." she trailed off as she walked away.

I flicked through the class pictures of every year from 1968, when my mother had braces and seemed a little flat-chested, to junior cheerleader, to her graduation, and then beyond. In the last volume, 1972, I spotted a familiar face in the tenth grade. *Danny Kent.* Same little smirk as my father, bigger nose. A brother, four years younger. I asked for the next couple of annuals and followed him through graduation, hair getting longer, becoming stoic, detached. Didn't play football. Sort of a stoner, guitar player, one frame of him with two other boys, on bass and drums, screwing their faces up, fingers a blur of motion, the caption, *Tolo 1973*. Kids were watching, not dancing. Some kids looked the other way. Not many kids in the gym at all. I wrote down the names of the other two boys—Jim Kenney, Buddy Gomez.

I went back to the '68 and '69 books. In the eleventh grade a shot of Mom dancing, slow-dancing, with Richard Nelson. So, they were friends, yearbook staffers. Maybe she felt sorry for him. A pity dance. Another photo in the back, they ended up next to each other in a group shot of the theatre club stage crew, cutting up, funny faces; one guy held a broom like a shotgun, another had a floodlight can. I picked up the magnifying glass chained to the Oxford Dictionary. Richard and Mom were holding hands.

I set up the laptop, logged onto the school internet, and tried to look up addresses or phone numbers of Kents but ran into pay-only websites. In the end I just used a phone book the librarian pulled from a bottom drawer, Google-mapped a couple of addresses and sketched them out. Three Palmers turned up. Two Kents. I started to Google the Nelsons as well, but the school was closing and the shy, fragile-looking high-school girl who had taken over the librarian's desk asked me to leave.

▬ ▬ ▬

The first address was in an apartment building, broken plastic toys scattered over foot-worn lawns of dog turds and junk food wrappers. I walked up to the second floor and knocked. A Hispanic girl answered the door.

"*Quién es usted?*" A baby sat on the floor behind her.

I was looking for somebody in their fifties at least. It didn't feel right. I apologized and left.

The second address was a mobile court, manicured like a cemetery, no trees, and sun glaring off the white metal like noon in Cairo. I drove around, passed someone in a golf cart, stopped at space number 138, a screened-in porch attached to the front of a white metal doublewide. An old couple sat in the shade of the porch watching a television I could hear from the street. The white-haired woman stood and met me at the door. I explained who I was looking for.

"My name *was* Kent, but I've remarried. This is Mr. Bemis."

The old man nodded, then gazed back at the TV.

"You can call me Millie. You must be looking for Kathy Kent's boys. She was my sister-in- law while I was married to Clyde. They split up years ago, about the time the boys finished school. Clyde's dead now—Honey, isn't Clyde dead?" Mr. Bemis nodded again but never looked away from his screen. "Kathy's down in Arizona somewhere, last I heard."

She motioned me to come in and gestured to a loveseat where an enormous yellow cat lay sleeping. "Jes' push him off of there." She sat down opposite me. "They weren't regular people, the two of them. Sorta wild." She sneezed and took a tissue from a box on the coffee table. "Boys growed up the same way." She blew her nose. "Older one went in the Army after some trouble with the law. Got himself killed I heard."

My eyes adjusted to the dark and I realized she had little statues—no, salt and pepper shakers, hundreds of them, on every available cabinet and along a little shelf circling the living room near the ceiling.

"Other boy—" She fell silent. "You know, it's shameful. They're not of my blood, but nephews nonetheless. Can't remember that boy's name."

"Danny?"

"Why yes. Daniel. Daniel tried to get me to send him some money, a couple of years ago." She stood and went to a small roll-top, pulled one bundle of envelopes, then another and another, snapping off the rubber bands, flipping through them until the desktop was almost covered and I was about to tell her to stop. "Here it is." She held it at arm's length and pulled her head back. "Whitefish." She handed it to me.

The writing looked like a child's, magic marker soaked into the paper rendering it almost unreadable. Just *Whitefish*. No street address. Maybe it was general delivery.

"You can keep that if it pleases you. You're closer to him than me."

I thanked her, tucking the letter in my shirt. We talked a while longer. No, she didn't know any Palmer girls and never heard of the older Kent boy getting married, but she lost track of them after high school.

- - -

At one of the addresses for Palmer, a girl answered the door in a business suit, just home from work, it appeared. Her husband was from Portland, and both of his parents were alive, last she checked. At the second address, on Harrison Hill, a plumbing truck pulled into the driveway just ahead of me. A black man got out, a small black girl running from the front door to greet him. At the last address, a nice rancher three miles from town with a long driveway, I was met by a very Italian-looking man, an old *nonnina* at the kitchen table. Said they'd just moved there, wanted to know why I wanted to know, and watched me leave through the curtains as I drove off. New Jersey plates on a big Cadillac by the side of the house.

It was after six and all I had was a partial address of an uncle I'd never seen, brother of a father I'd never known. Some guy who could barely write, who, even in his fifties, I estimated, had to resort to begging an old woman for money. Maybe he was a cripple. Maybe a vet like myself but couldn't put two and two together anymore. The VA was full of guys like that, all of them some mother's son with a life of dreams before them, long ago, that never came true. I would talk to him until something connected. He'd look at me and know I was his brother's boy.

Evening was falling, so I drove down I-82, avoiding the desolate back country and all of the voices there, crossing the shallow river in wide sweeps of the highway, dense stands of trees near the water's edge, long shadows cast across rows of hop vines stretching across the valley, hills still rich and warm with sunlight. At a few points men stood in the river with their sons, fishing.

At a Super 8 I took a first-floor room looking out at a courtyard, a dozen or so little kids, all squeals and pool toys and wet faces, and thought about that morning. *Those kinds of delusions happen*, I realized, *when I'm idle*. Give me a mission and my mind doesn't start putting things together out of pieces of shit.

The TV seemed to be all survival shows, people doing their worst to each other, everybody sort of a prick. Life has no good guys, they were telling me. Just survivors. Would like to put a helmet cam on each one of them and throw their ass out the back of a Chinook over Jalalabad, see how they survive.

When my almond chicken arrived I gave the guy a ten and ate next to the window with a glass of ice water, trying to make sense of Danny Kent's letter. I opened my bag after that, took each of my evening meds and turned out the light, the sky outside still pale gray, falling asleep to the splashing, the flutter of children's voices, the sounds that children make before they learn to bully, or want, or feel hate or jealousy.

5

A cocktail napkin was wedged near my doorknob when I got home the following afternoon, *CALL ME* in ballpoint. I dumped my suitcase on the futon, went over and knocked on her door. No answer.

I sat at my kitchen table and unfolded Danny Kent's letter again.

I worked for the forrest survice, helped put out that fire near Calispell. Then: *les scwabb, learned that getting my hands dirty was ok . . . built an apartment house in Boner's fairy.* He seemed to be giving his work history—his start history, anyway—at a half-dozen positions, badly misspelled but with a bravado of accomplishment, and I wondered why he lost all those jobs. Debbie, whoever she was, had left because *she could not keep the faith.* In the last sentence he asked Millie to send him $3,000, *money order would be best*, reasoning *we are of one God, one Family.*

Aunt Millie, and it gave me a small degree of comfort to call her that, hadn't said, but I got the feeling she didn't send him a cent. I wasn't sure I could sympathize with a guy who quoted the Psalms to shake down an old lady.

Then I started to appreciate how lucky I had been to have one employer for fifteen years, food and board—how rare that could be for a lot of guys, even during the Eighties. How I couldn't land a permanent job with my associate's degree when I was out. It could be really tough, and I was being an asshole. *Construction jobs end all the time,* I reasoned. Debbie leaving him could have spun him out of orbit for a while. I was still going to have to talk to him eventually; maybe I should brush up on my Psalms.

- - -

A tap at the door. Her tap. I'm learning her tap.

"You didn't call me." She stood arms crossed, pushing her breasts up in her tank top.

"I don't have your number," I said. "You didn't call me either."

"You never gave me your number."

"I rest my case." I turned away, back to my seat at the kitchen table, leaving the door open so she could follow.

"Thought you might be out drinking with your big macho Army buddies. I missed you." She rubbed my shoulders briefly, then swiveled into the opposite chair. "You didn't come home last night."

"Nope."

"Where'd you stay?"

"I had to go down to the Yakima Valley. Sunnyside."

She crossed her arms and her cleavage rose again. "Don't tell me you got a girl, in *Sunnyside?*"

"It's complicated."

"I bet."

"Look, I don't have any macho Army buddies. I wish I did. And I slept in a motel. In Richland."

"By yourself?"

"I think there were about a hundred other people registered too. What are we? Going steady?"

All the starch went out of her. "Guys. All alike."

I pushed my chair back. "I'm trying to find my grandparents, okay?"

"Why not ask your folks?"

"They're dead." This startled her, like no one our age was supposed to have dead parents. She reached for my hands, but I swung them behind me. "Long time ago. Not a big deal."

"But you're just now looking?"

"I've been busy." I could say that my psychiatrist told me to do this, but she didn't need to know that. I felt scrutinized, invaded. You shouldn't feel like that with someone you've slept with, had sex with. I was just learning about pop-ups on my laptop, how intrusive they could be. I started to feel the same way about her. A thump came from the wall followed by exuberant giggling. We both turned. "Kids home?"

"Yeah. Sounds like I better get back." She stood up, the scent of musk oil, roses, drifting past.

I caught her hand. "Still want to fix me dinner?"

"Not much in the fridge right now."

I plunged my other hand into my pocket, brought out two twenties. "Surprise me. I'm easy."

"I'll put the kids to bed about eight. Sometime after?"

"Sounds good."

She started to leave.

"I missed you too, Jennifer. And the lizard."

She twirled with a big grin and spun away.

■ ■ ■

She broiled a fillet of salmon with some crushed nuts, and sautéed asparagus. Bottle of Barefoot Chardonnay. Two candles, each half burned down, in molded glass candlesticks. The children's unfinished mac and cheese still visible on the counter; they giggled from their bedroom and kept peeking down the hallway until she went to their room and, after a few minutes of silence, returned and sat down.

I refilled her glass. "Duct tape?"

"That's cruel. I just read them a story." She set her plate aside and scooted her chair closer. "You have any kids anywhere?"

"That I know about?"

"Don't be cheap."

"I was married once, for about two years. No kids."

"Tell me a war story then."

"About my marriage?"

She smirked. "No, silly. About what you did. Over there."

I halted right there. I thought about my last talk with Zilker, and it would put a cold wetness on the whole evening. She was wearing a white tube top and cutoffs, low-heeled sandals, some perfume that sent all kinds of signals, and I wanted exactly what she wanted, I thought, and she didn't really know that all the stuff in my head could give her and her children nightmares for years.

"We lived in these barracks, sort of pop-up huts. Like the Quonset huts in old war movies, but smaller. With insulation."

"The round things." She scooted closer. "The round things," she repeated.

"And there were eight of us in there, a squad." I laughed. "And some of 'em, most of them, they snore. I used to try to breathe out when they snored, like it wouldn't be as loud."

"Eight is a lot of guys."

And I could tell by how she wrinkled her nose that it sounded stinky to her. "There's eight guys in a squad, unless one of them gets killed."

She went silent.

"But nobody—" And I thought of Marsden then, and an RPG right in his stomach that didn't go off, and him lying against a wall, his face all screwed up in a scream, but he couldn't because it hurt too much to breathe, and you could see the fins sticking out just below his vest, and if it had hit the vest it would have gone off, killed him right then, and probably the blast would have gotten the two of us closest to him. Garcia crawled over and just pulled it out and laid it there, and then you could tell it occurred to him it still might go off, and he dragged Marsden back through a doorway and dumped a couple of quick clots in the hole, but they just floated away and we all started stuffing in every bit of packing from our kits, Marsden beginning to get it, that this wasn't good, and he was looking at my face, then

Garcia's, back and forth with that big question and wanting to read something that we weren't going to give him, just staying busy, poker-faced, then Marsden getting quieter and quieter. Chopper was there in eighteen minutes, but I knew he was dead when we loaded him, all of his blood in the dirt and looking like we'd cleaned a deer there. "Nobody in my platoon ever got killed, okay?"

"Yeah. Okay." She stepped behind me and massaged my shoulders. "You're so tense. Got just what you need." She reached over the cabinet above the refrigerator, laid a Ziploc on the table.

"Pot?"

She tossed some papers on the table.

"I really can't do that."

"Come on. We're going to have a lot of fun," she singsonged, swaying side to side.

"You go ahead." I remembered my medication. "I'll be right back."

At my apartment I found a Vistaril, took half of a Viagra, and stood looking at the wall, imagining her through the plaster rolling a tight little joint. Pulling it through her mouth to wet it a bit. We used to patrol with the ANA. We were supposed to be training them. For fuck's sake, we had to train them to put their helmets on the right way; sometimes they'd be backwards. Most of them stoned all the time. Break ranks in a firefight and charge, or scatter, and we spend half a day burying them. Too fucked up to know if their AK was loaded. Hashish use was just another kind of suicide for a soldier and everybody with him. Stoned people get too focused on themselves, no empathy; your leg is blown open and they say "Bummer, man," and go back to staring at a little bump on the back of their hand. If our own guys were found with the stuff, even on liberty, somebody would bust them up, put them in the infirmary, even break an arm. You didn't want somebody like that in the field with you.

I thought about her tan and what she wanted and tried to put all of it out of my mind. Just for tonight, I thought, maybe she'll learn something from me. When I got back to the table she was waiting. She'd rolled two.

"You go ahead," I said. "You're used to it." Downed the rest of my wine. "Might mess with my medications."

"You know you can cook with it, too." She gestured at the remaining salmon, flecked with nuts and dark green specks.

"That's not parsley?"

She shook her head slowly, sweetly, satanic.

"I don't feel any different."

"You will."

The tiniest wave of anger rose in me, betrayal, then evaporated like steam from a mirror; I forgot what I was going to say.

She took a long drag, held it a few seconds, then blew a smoke ring. "You were going to tell me a war story."

I smiled, leaned back in my chair, shook my head. The room swayed in increments.

She got a serious expression, took another drag and held it while the sweep hand on the kitchen clock made three quarters of a rotation. When she exhaled she squeaked, "Please?" Then giggled.

"I can't tell you one because it would be a lie. Do you understand?" We both leaned over the table, inches from each other, her eyes like bright little motors. "War doesn't have a beginning or an end, or any kind of plot, you see?"

She nodded.

"Just a bunch of scary chaos. A lot of boredom in between. So, if I tried to tell a *story*, something would have to be made up."

She began to stroke my face like I was a puppy.

"People want to hear *stories* to be entertained."

She kissed the side of my mouth.

"War just doesn't come close." I took her face in my palms. "You have any of your paintings you could show me?"

"Drawings. Pen and ink." She pushed her hair back from her face. "It's been a long time." She went to the hall closet, dug around for a few minutes, tossing backpacks and shoes and a folding stroller onto the carpet behind her. "Here." She laid a lopsided plaster oval on the table. "Brenna made this in pottery class."

It looked like a try at a bowl, or an ashtray, rainbows of color spread with fingertips, unfired plaster. "That's pretty good. And pretty, too." I held it closer to the candle. "I thought you were going to show me your drawings."

"Oh yeah." She rotated a finger at her temple. "Silly me."

She went back to the hall closet, stared at it quizzically for a moment, then disappeared into the bedroom. A few thumps, the roll of a closet door. "Why don't you come back here," she called.

A candle was lit on the nightstand. A CD played soft, throaty harp music. She'd unzipped a portfolio and opened it, covering most of her bed; a stack of drawing paper, frayed at the corners, fanned like a hand of cards; the top sheet a pencil sketch, edges marred by eraser—a girl with two braids, determined, solemn. I looked at it, then looked at her.

"We all had to do a self-portrait." She flipped it over. "Didn't mean for you to see that one."

"It's good," I said, and turned it over again. "You were so serious."

"I was eighteen." She stared at the face impassively. "I don't think I drew teeth very well."

We flipped through the folder, one sheet after another, and she stopped longer on a few, on some with a start, as if she'd never seen them before, or had but meant to discard them. A still-life of flowers. A staircase leading to a black doorway. A wooded road, tangles of branches. We stopped at a garden scene, floods of transparent yellows and orange and violet. "I tried to watercolor that one." She dragged a finger over it. "Never finished it."

"It's not too late," I said. I spotted a little red triangle near the center. "You put a gnome in there!"

"Yeah. You've got an eye for detail. Instructor never even saw it. Or didn't say anything if she did." She smiled, looking at the forgotten sheet. "Two more, I think. Can you find them too?"

I studied it for a moment and found two tiny figures, at the edge, crawling beneath a fence. I pointed them out.

"Very astute." She closed the portfolio carefully but then

tossed it on the floor beneath the window. The sheets fluttered out, scattered across the carpet. "Long time ago." She turned off the bedside lamp and closed the bedroom door.

"You could get a book, an easel," I said, but she was against me, her tongue just above my collarbone.

"So, what did you really do, in the Army?" She started to unbutton my shirt.

"I had to find gnomes," I whispered. "Bad gnomes with guns, so far away nobody else could see them."

She tugged at my belt buckle, giggling and growling.

"I had to shoot their little caps off."

She spread her fingers inside the waist of my jeans and slid them down, pushed me back on the bed and fell upon me, her tongue, her mouth on every angle of my body. I arched, neck over the edge of the mattress in speechless euphoria, while her nails traced the length of my torso, fell into the small of my back. The vacuum of her lips, the ballet of her tongue might've swallowed me altogether, and I wanted her to. A small gnome looked up at me from the floor in the flicker of the candlelight.

"Too late, too late," she whispered.

- - -

Something was in my nose—delicate, inquisitive antennae. Then my ear, then a firm little tug and a shot of torment. I opened my eyes and the gnome was there, a corona of light around his head. No, a little boy, his fingers embedded in my earlobe.

"Are you our new dad?"

Jennifer groaned under the covers. "Casey, go to your room."

"Hungry."

"Mommy will get up and make breakfast soon. Go play with Benny-bunny. Don't wake up your sister."

I closed my eyes to the glare and listened to little feet waddle away.

"Sorry," she said. "I should have locked the door." She sat up. "Fuck. It's eight thirty."

"You have to be at work?"

"Pre-school. I'll just say they were sick." She looked at the drawings scattered over the floor. Casey had stepped on one, tearing it a little. "Shit," she whispered, and turned to me with the same morning-after hesitation I'd seen on her face three days before. I was part of the mess she had to clean up. "So, you were a sniper."

"You could say that."

"Shot people that didn't even see it coming."

"Nobody ever sees it coming." I took her hand and tried to joke. "If they did they'd just duck."

She pulled away. "It's not funny."

"You're right, it's not. But it was my job."

"For twenty years?"

"Fifteen. And not even that. Just while I was in Afghanistan. Jennifer, everybody I shot had a gun. Every one of those guys would have killed ten or twenty American soldiers." I stood, pulled my pants on. "I saved 400, maybe 800 guys. A lot of them eighteen or nineteen."

"So that's the way you look at it?"

"I thought you said a girl feels safe around a guy that can kill someone if they need to."

"I never said that. Never!"

She was right, I thought. It was Kaye.

"Any one of those guys could be saying the same thing, how many people they saved, to their sweetheart." She glared at me. "If they were still alive." She pulled on her bra. Her eyes narrowed. "Eight hundred? How many men did you kill?"

"Forty-three."

She stopped still. "You kept count?"

"The Army did. Probably a whole lot more."

"I can't deal with this. Not right now." She stepped around me and started to make the bed.

"I was with the good guys, remember?" My voice tightened, trying to calm myself, knowing I should leave.

"I'm sure they thought the same thing." She turned. "Most of them were just farmers, you know, don't have all this high-techno stuff that you probably used. Shit, you're no better than those bastards who sit in Nebraska, kill people with drones."

I had her by the neck, the throat, in a moment, her right hand twisted up between her shoulder blades, my face an inch from hers. "We didn't crash airplanes into their cities. Remember?" She was gasping, eyes bulging, righteous vindication all over her puffy red face. I pushed her away and she fell onto the bed, wriggling back to the headboard.

"Maybe we had it coming. Asshole." Her voice cracked, a sob before I slammed the door behind me.

- - -

I paced my apartment several times, feeling like I was wearing someone else's clothes, then walked down to the 7-Eleven and bought a pint of chocolate milk and drank it on the way back, unbalanced, noises way too loud, the sun too awful. Chocolate milk was one of those things that made me feel better when I was a kid, but it didn't help that much. It used to come in a carton with soft paper edges; now it was in a plastic bottle and didn't taste right.

I felt set up, sold out, ambushed, but absolutely horrible about grabbing her like that, certainly not how I was trained, not by the book, not a civilian, and she'd become the enemy in a heartbeat. Not how a good soldier *soldiers*. For a moment she probably thought I was going to kill her. I know that I wouldn't have, but she didn't. *The wound from a gun will heal, the wound from the tongue does not*; another proverb I brought home.

Fucking pot. Would have to avoid any piss tests for a month or so. Totally fucks with your situational awareness.

Never had much chance to get into the drug culture. Mr. Dunham, I'd figured, could smell drugs as well as any of those checkpoint dogs. There wasn't any meth at the high school then, either. I read Carlos Castaneda, a book that had been Mrs. Dunham's in college, all about eating hallucinogenic mushrooms and becoming enlightened, and I didn't take much away from the book because I knew I was already enlightened, watching my mother slowly embalm herself, and taking a substance to heighten reality was so much bullshit. I do remember, however, *finding one's place.* A truism that maybe some Buddhist wandering by whispered in Carlos's ear while he was stoned, and he attributed it to the mushrooms. It stayed with me all these years. In Iraq, in college, at Fort Benning, in the brush in Afghanistan, it was like a religion for me, finding my place. A kind of balance there, to take a shot, or sleep, or find a place in a room with other guys. Next to Jennifer was *not* my place. I knew this all along and deliberately overlooked it; selfish of me, but I just wanted to have her and now I felt even more ashamed of myself. She must have known it too. She just wanted me to be what she was looking for, a copy of herself. And she wanted to fuck me. And I wanted to fuck her and actually remember it this time. Two greedy people. I wanted to apologize but didn't even know where to start because she wouldn't see it like I did.

Sniper school taught me patience. Hours of thought, careful observation, and the occasional exchange with your spotter. The spotter could be the voice of reason as well. Jordan would lie there with his spotting scope, which had a wider angle of view. He sensed body language between the men we watched that I couldn't get with my narrower field; he could distinguish harmless intent from malicious. Sometimes we'd come back without taking any targets. I miss that sense of perseverance. Seems like nothing in this life calls for it—everybody shoots from the hip, so busy texting and complaining, we don't look at each other anymore.

"Just farmers," she'd said. All caught up in rooting for the little guy, probably watched all the *Star Wars* movies. Sometimes the little guy is one nasty bastard that will rape your wife before he guts her, disembowel your baby daughter, peel the skin off your face while you're still alive. She didn't *believe* in guns. Like saying she didn't *believe* in concrete, or eggplants.

I reached the apartments and her car was still there, so I walked another couple of blocks and wondered what conversation had unfolded before her previous boyfriend put his fist through the wall.

It was almost ten. I took my morning pill and threw a backpack in the trunk with the Gerber and a change of clothes. Whitefish was about 250 miles away, an easy four-hour drive. I could be there by three in the afternoon local time, spend a couple of hours at the post office or the county assessor's office. Maybe the auditor's office. I looked at my laptop on the seat. It might be in there, on the web somewhere.

Now I was on a mission. I function best when I have a point to work toward, after which I can say "that's done," or look at order restored, stuff where it belongs, where it will help. Threat removed. Understand the mission, identify the target, preparation, execution. There's not a lot of difference between taking the garbage out and taking out a hostile. I looked around me, at the homes along the highway, and it occurred to me not everyone had their mission down. Some little ranches nice and tidy, other places surrounded by disabled cars and rusting farm equipment, bristling with spines and levers, cockeyed old mobile homes, sheds with metal roofs flapping in the wind, horses standing in shit beneath their shelter. Maybe some single drunk mother in there, raising a fifteen-year-old boy.

Maybe they had too many missions. Or too many distractions. Or too much TV, or too many people telling them their lives were shit and somebody else was supposed to take out their garbage. Or their kids were fucking up, drinking, doing drugs, getting pregnant—too many disasters in too many directions. Perhaps that's how Julia's parents thought we would end up, so they did their best to hustle me out the door. Some of the old guys on the ward talked about their families that way. Eventually, the kids end up running the farm, sometimes over a cliff. It was a painful way of thinking and made my head hurt. Made me wish I was back in, with *my* family, *my kids*.

Every other car or truck had a yellow ribbon stuck somewhere on the back, and it got annoying. How many of them really contributed to some cause for vets? Most of them just gave some pathetic amputee outside a grocery store a buck to make themselves feel better. Want to support our troops? Give us a purpose when we come back, give us a job that matters, at least a fraction of the one we just gave up, a place where we belong. Then leave us the fuck alone. Stop treating us like cerebral palsy kids.

- - -

Divided highways are always a relief; something goes down, it's on the other side of that space and moving the other direction. I keep my distance from the cars ahead, a hundred yards minimum. Shrapnel slows down a lot in that distance, but it fucking unnerves me when people get right on my ass and stay there, or just over my shoulder and won't pass. I'll check my mirror—*Are they rolling down the windows?*

It was almost one, and I realized my head was pounding because I hadn't eaten anything since the chocolate milk that morning. I turned into Plains, Montana, and made a sharp left into the first restaurant that advertised *Breakfast Served All Day*. I sat in the car and tucked my shirt, looked the place over for a moment. Blue and white and peeling clapboard siding, probably hadn't been painted since the interstate went through.

A woman stepped down from a gunmetal-gray diesel Ford, maybe her husband's, crossed the parking lot, hair a storm of walnut and honey curls, windblown and thick.

She might have been in her thirties or forties, had a nice chin, and a black Velcro brace wrapped around her right knee. A healthy pair of Wranglers, and boots worn buff with just a bit of a heel. Her posture, her stride even as she limped, spoke all kinds of confidence. I reached the door just before her and could see some pain as she swung her right leg up on the step.

My own knee was rigid from the drive. "We should be on *Limping with the Stars*." I held the door open for her.

She turned and regarded me indifferently, maybe expecting someone she knew, and didn't answer, but took a menu from the hostess, who seemed to know her and seated her immediately. A few minutes later I was shown to my own table and, after limping back from the restroom, opened my menu.

"Excuse me." She sat facing me, one table over beyond a table-height partition dividing the dining room. "What was that you said to me, at the door?"

"I said, 'We should both be on *Limping with the Stars*.' Dumb joke. Sorry."

She puckered, then smiled briefly, and little laughter lines formed at her eyes. "No. That's good. That's real good."

"What happened to your leg?"

"Horse fell on it, a couple of months ago. It's getting better. Yours?"

"Infection. Some kind of fungus from Afghanistan. Turned out to be a real cluster."

The waitress brought her coffee and she stirred in two creamers and a packet of sugar.

"You were going to say clusterfuck, weren't you?"

I nodded. "Too long in the Army."

"My father used to say that all the time. And FUBAR, and SNAFU, and BUFF. I was an Air Force brat."

"He's gone now?"

"No, just had a stroke. Still gets around pretty well but can't talk. Now he says 'Quafer-fuh.' He used to scare me when he got mad. Now it's kind of entertaining."

"Hope *Dancing with the Stars* isn't a favorite."

She shook her head. "Don't even own a TV. My daughter watches it at a friend's house. You?"

"Don't own one either. Watched whatever was on in the hospital. Tabloids always talking about it at checkout stands."

She had strong hands, nails painted warm red but short, arms tanned up to the elbows. She set a bundle of mail on the tabletop, opened a pen knife and started slicing each envelope.

An old man wandered between the tables, carrying a coffee can and a bundle of red silk poppies, dressed in a uniform that might have been from World War II. DAV charity. When he came to my table I palmed him a dollar and he laid the flower in front of me. I sat twirling it between my fingers, then reached over the partition and placed it on her mail.

"Why thank you. You don't like poppies?"

"I spent a whole summer in Helmand province. Taliban spent half their time trying to kill me, other half growing poppies."

"But you bought one from him anyway."

I shrugged. "Only thing he had to offer, I guess."

She glanced sidelong, a half-smile.

My omelet came and we both ate quietly. I took in all of her—the gray-flecked tangle of hair, pulled back now in a band, Carhart vest, denim blouse, the piece of turquoise around her neck on a strand of leather, the quick scan of her eyes on each page unfolded—not really meaning to stare, but eventually she caught my glance.

"Sorry. Have a lot of accounts to catch up on. Rude of me."

"Not sure I'm always the best conversationalist."

"There's a time for everything, they say. Even staring at a woman you've just met." The waitress brought her ticket and she put a credit card in the folder. She turned to me again. "Just kidding you. Cheryl Redding." She extended her hand, a solid handshake.

"Robert Kent." I almost said Robby. Not sure why I didn't.

"Usually there's some bills here in town, and instead of mailing checks I just walk around and pay them. Catch up on gossip. And you?"

"Going up to Whitefish. Found out I have an uncle up there I didn't know about."

"Your parents never said anything?"

"Dad's brother. I never knew my dad."

"My daughter's never known hers."

"Mine went missing in Vietnam."

"So you *really* don't know." She sipped her coffee, took a long time to swallow. "That's a lot to carry around."

"I've carried worse, probably. Just trying to dig up some history before I move forward. And your daughter?"

She smiled, a question on her lips that she didn't ask, and didn't answer me. She stood, gathered her mail, and wrapped the wire stem of the poppy around one of the snaps near her lapel. She slipped a card from her purse. "If you get tired of digging and want to see a real old-fashioned dude ranch right out of the Fifties, stop by sometime." She put the card on my table:

Harbour Ranch, Vacation Rentals and Retreat.
Robert and Cheryl Redding

"Robert's my dad's name too." She gave a quick smile. "It's a good name." And she turned and walked out.

I watched her traverse the parking lot, where she tossed some of her mail on the front seat of the Ford, then disappeared into a crowd at the crosswalk. I looked for her across the street but couldn't spot her again. I folded an unused napkin, *Heather's Country Kitchen*, over the card and shoved it in my shirt pocket.

- - -

Mom used to talk about how Dad would come home someday, just walk up to the trailer and let himself in. I used to picture that, and he was always in his class A when he did. As I grew up I imagined what he'd look like as he aged, like those missing persons on TV where the artist sketched what they might look like twenty years later. On the drive to Whitefish, all those imaginings came back with a tremendous sense of arrival. Getting close.

- - -

"Even if there were ten Danny Kents in Flathead County, I couldn't tell you where they were if I wanted to," the auditor's clerk apologized. "So you've got the same last name. I believe your story, but the system isn't indexed that way." He closed his registry. "You got to have at least a plat number."

I had searched the phone books first. Nothing, but then again almost everybody has a cell phone now. I was sitting in the archives of the *Whitefish Pilot*, looking up births and weddings, when a baseball-capped policeman stepped in, tossed an envelope on the counter. "Week's records." He touched his brim and stepped out.

"Thanks, Bill," the receptionist called after him.

I sat for a minute astounded by my naïveté. That was it, and I'd glossed right over it. My uncle, colorful as he seemed, would have a police record. Something trivial, probably.

I went to the counter and posed my question, and she hesitated but came to my monitor and clicked a different tab: *Public Records*.

Danny Kent, a.k.a. Daniel Kent, could have occupied an entire hard drive alone. Seventeen parking violations. Three DUIs. Eleven assaults. Contributing to the delinquency of a minor— two violations. Carrying a handgun into a public building. Hunting on public land without a license—four violations. Taking deer out of season—two violations. Possession with intent to deliver, three citations. Seven failures to appear. Twice urinating in public. All of it in the last eight years.

Assault. Hard to picture exactly what that meant. Did he pick out a friendly and cut loose on them? Or just disputes with fellow drunks? Address 12400 Cedar Lake Road. Maybe he lived on a lake. Couldn't be that difficult a guy to communicate with. I had smoothed the hackles of more than one old Afghan patriarch carrying an AK-47. It's body language—keep your horns covered, don't look too much at their eyes. Come up with a proverb or two. I could talk to anyone. And this guy was *family*.

The next morning, I checked out of my motel and headed north to Cedar Lake Road, gaining altitude, passing an occasional address sign or a wicket over a drive, sometimes a steel cutout of a cowboy with a mailbox welded to it, the silent foothills of the Rockies watching over me in the distance, peaks veiled in slow-moving storm. Collapsed barn in a pasture, a doublewide near the road here and there. If the county had assigned addresses, very few of them belonged to anybody. The pavement turned to gravel, and I slowed where *13105* appeared on a small placard nailed to a power pole next to a gravel drive. I made a three-point and retraced the last quarter mile, found *11400* marked in reflective letters next to another drive, the name *Waters* just below. I turned in and rounded a bend to a small metal barn and a two-story farmhouse from the Thirties. In the small pasture adjacent, a herd of brown-and-white Nubian goats, a boy herding them. As I slowed he sank into the grass. A bull-chested, white-haired man was dragging hay bales onto the back of a flatbed.

He came over to the window when I rolled it down. "Yeah?"

"You know a Danny Kent that lives in this area?"

"You a bail bondsman?"

"No. They come by a lot?"

"Sheriff's just over there a bit. He's an odd type." He took off his work gloves and pointed. "Go back out to the road, take a left, then turn left at the second drive you come to. Really just a break in the fence."

"How far to his house?" I watched the goats but the boy never reappeared.

The man squatted down so we were eye level. "I ain't never seen his house. Might live in a teepee for all I know. But you go in there, he'll find you." He started to stand again. "He's not too sociable. You go over there, be real, real careful."

At the break in the fence there were two furrows in the earth, and after a hundred feet or so they vanished into two depressions in the deep pasture grass. I rolled along in the Corolla until it was clear I'd be boxed in by dead scrub and killed the engine. I slid the Gerber into the top of my boot, pulled my BDUs over it and got out. The ground was uneven, as if it had been tilled and then allowed to grow over. The midday heat poured across the field, the back of my neck, my scalp; insects launched like spring darts from the weeds. Even the trees smelled hot. I had walked about fifteen minutes uphill when a twig snapped off to my right and I dropped instinctively, no weapon to shoulder.

"You're trespassin'."

"I need to talk to you," I called.

Silence.

I repeated myself, louder. The grass muffled my voice, and my notion of bonding on the basis of family was crumbling already.

"You are *tress . . . passing.*"

"I know I'm trespassing. We need to talk." I lifted my head a few inches. "I think we're related."

He stood near the tree line, fifty feet away, empty-handed. "You can stand up and do your talking right there. I ain't gonna shoot you or nothin'." Dressed in a worn work shirt and denim jacket, a messianic mop of gray hair and beard. Sunglasses.

"I'm Robby Kent. Your brother was my father. I think."

He crept forward a few steps, his arms undulating in exaggerated wonder, but he was already flanking me a little, and I turned to stay face-on. "That so?" He stepped closer, leaning forward, searching for detail in my buttons, or scent, then stepped back and viewed me as a whole. "I guess there's some resemblance."

The wind shifted abruptly, and I smelled him—cigarettes, wood smoke, diesel and body odor—and began to have doubts. There was sarcasm in his voice, in his body language, but I decided some people just used that as a defense, confronted by strangers.

"My father was Andrew Kent. He was—"

"I know who he was. Killed in Nam." He stepped beside me and touched me on the elbow. "Why don't you and I head on up to the house, talk about this." He walked next to me, which felt evenhanded.

"How old are you?"

"Thirty-five."

"So you were born in '72?"

"Yeah. July 30th." We entered the woods. "Your brother met my mom in high school."

"That so?"

His arm swung, a metallic blur. The base of my skull exploded.

— — —

I vomited when I woke up and he rolled me to one side. "Don't want you choking on your puke. Just yet."

My neck and scalp felt scalded, pressed against cold, moist sand, the sun in a halo behind his head as he breathed down. I was lying in a shallow grave, wrists and ankles bound.

He twirled a roll of duct tape over my head. "Good thing I didn't tape your mouth." He cleared his throat, spat close to my head. "I knowed who you were when you come in. Watched you the whole time." He squatted halfway, swinging an arm to the horizon. "I knowed exactly who you were." He knelt closer, snapped my VIC card under my nose. "You're from the government!"

I realized then I couldn't feel my wallet under my butt cheek anymore. "That's my veteran's card, you dumb fuck!"

He swayed back and stood up. "Don't talk dirty to me now."

I wriggled, trying to pull my ankles up near my wrists.

He smiled, sardonic. "I got your little knife, too." He waved the Gerber and gave it a toss. "You talk dirty. Gonna pay." Straddle-legged, unzipping his pants, moments later he urinated in my face, my eyes, nose, some went into my throat and I coughed. He zipped up and squatted again. "We're going to be respectful, aren't we?"

I didn't answer, dumbstruck.

"Say it! We're going to be respectful."

My throat stung of urine and I answered hoarsely. "I can't fucking believe I spent fifteen years of my life fighting for crazy assholes like you to piss on people."

"Don't tell me about that. *Nooooo*, don't you dare. My brother—" And he began to turn in circles, pursuing some equation of circular logic. "My brother." He pointed at me. "My brother gave everything. Everything. Everything!" And he circled more intently, stomping, chanting, "My brother! My brother! My brother! I have bowed down in mourning as one who bewhailith his mother!" He stopped, his face full of creative enlightenment, amazed that he had rhymed something. He squatted again. "You going to be respectful?"

"Sure."

"For I am beneath the Lord and you are beneath me and you shall tell, for thy days"—and he looked at his watch and snorted—"shit, for thy *minutes* are numbered."

I spat more urine-sand out of my mouth. "I'm not going to tell."

He froze, eyes whipping nervously. "But it's my duty to wrest forth the truth. My duty to the others." He paused again, looked into the brush in several directions with cautious concern that he had betrayed some secret.

"Who are the others, Danny?" I didn't really care at that point, but I seemed to have touched a nerve.

He looked down at me as if he'd momentarily forgotten I was there. "How clever is the beast." He made a fist, hovered over me, picking a target, then crushed the left side of my jaw.

Blood erupted in my mouth and I pushed a tooth back in place with my tongue. "Shit! Break my jaw I'm not going to be able to tell you shit!"

"Shit?" He quieted. "Shit?" He stood and turned, dropped his denims.

I lurched away as he farted forcefully, runny yellow stool dripping into the sand where my head had been.

He turned, a little crestfallen. "That's not like me." He reached in my shirt pocket, took the napkin and card and wiped himself. "You see"—he pulled his pants up—"my brother an' me, we both had our cords cut, you know. In Seattle. I remember 'cuz I was eighteen and that's an important year. Andy, he was twenty. So he never had any fuckin' kids." He stood, circled the hole, kicked sand. "So you're a fuckin' liar." He grew more agitated and stomped around the hole in a kind of war dance, greasy hair flopping, beard swinging, then stopped, breathless. "You were sent here, weren't you? And now you're going to tell me all about them." And he pointed skyward. A dark blue tattoo of a cross adorned his left forearm; it looked self-inflicted.

He hopped away. Behind us I saw a shed—his house, I supposed—and he ducked inside. When I opened my eyes after a long blink he was there again, a large serrated survival knife in his hands, cheap China steel, and he fell on me, knees in my shoulders, the knife downturned, the point of it, smeared with some mucoid residue, scraping my chest.

"You will be buried in this hole. Do you not recognize it?" His breath as foul as the dribble of stool he'd released. "I am of the Shining Path." He drew the blade across my left arm, lightly, and a red plume unfolded like a flower.

I gritted my teeth. "You're not in the Shining Path. They're communists, Danny. Don't you know?" And suddenly we were speaking the same language, landed in the same zone.

He backed away, newly incensed, his entire theatric disrupted. "I'm not a communist," he said. He tugged at my feet, lifted them.

"Of course not. You're the brother of a patriot."

And he was dragging me. At the base of his steps I saw a wasp nest, covered with wasps, above his doorway. With each tug, the doorframe shook and the nest wiggled, and I was very concerned, briefly, that it was going to fall on my face.

Inside was cool. He left me on the floor for a few minutes while he caught his breath, broad ribcage heaving under thin skin where his shirt had come out, the place above his collar bones sucking in. He stood finally and, grasping beneath my arms, pulled me into a chair, leveling a finger.

"Now. You are going to tell me." He pulled a pair of pliers from his hip pocket and leaned forward.

I started to say "Wha—"

He grabbed my jaw, shit-stained fingers on my tongue. I think he was going to pull my teeth.

I bit him, then broke his nose with my forehead.

He screamed and dropped the pliers. I lunged forward, our combined weight crumpling his chair. I lurched and slammed and tried to roll, hit him with my head again, but my feet were over him and so I slammed—*wham, wham*—heels anywhere they could go, aiming for throat. Eventually I hit his chest and felt ribs crack. I stopped and looked at him. His face was bloody and I'd broken his sunglasses; saw his eyes, bleached blue, little rings of gray around pinpoint pupils. Gasping, a shark dragged onto the beach. He tried to sit up and I inch-wormed away, pushing my back up the wall. The knife lay on the arm of a sofa. I sat, back to it, and grasped, cutting the tape around my ankles.

He tried to sit, then rose to an unsteady stand. I side-kicked his knee and he went down with a scream. A few more manipulations of the knife eventually nicked the tape on my wrist enough to tear it loose.

"You broke my goddamned knee."

"Should have thought of that before you pissed on my face." My wallet lay on the table, all of my cards laid out like solitaire. I gathered those and inventoried the room, limping around, flies rising in clouds around me. Cartons of cigarettes crammed in an open cabinet, canned soup and chili and cases of beer occupied almost all remaining storage. The table was littered with small pieces of burnt foil, a mini-torch, a couple of asthma inhalers, baggies with white residue hugging the seams, and a Bible open to Deuteronomy, a glass pipe lying in the fold. I looked in the cover of the Bible, thinking it might have a family tree, but there were no markings. An old Fender guitar was wedged between his mattress and the wall, several strings gone. I tugged it loose.

"You play this?"

"Not anymore."

"You should get some strings. Would be good for you."

I looked in his bathroom and decided it might be better to piss outside. An AK-47 stood next to the door, another behind the drapery at the end of the couch. An AR-15 in the closet, a couple thousand rounds of ammunition, 7.62x39, .223, and 7.62x25. "Where's the pistol, Danny?"

"You broke my knee." He looked at the nightstand.

"It's just a ligament."

I opened the drawer at the bedside, picked out a Tokarev and shoved it in my belt. Beneath it, a badly scratched picture of my father in uniform, the same photo I'd grown up with.

I held it up. "I have this picture too." Nothing registered on his face; I'm not sure he could even identify it.

I rummaged in the drawer and found a spare magazine. Too much to carry. I popped the dust cover off one AK, pulled the piston out, then repeated it on the other. I dropped the bolt from the AR. All of them were thick with fouling. "These aren't very clean, Danny." I looked over. "Of course, neither are you. Tempting to burn this whole place down, you in it."

Outside, I located the Gerber and marched toward where I thought I'd parked, head still pounding, urine on my breath.

No keys. I had left them in the ignition, I was sure, in case I needed to leave quickly. I tossed the gun parts on the seat and trudged back to the house, trying to guess where along the path he'd hit me with the rifle butt. He wasn't a very strong guy, too short of breath there at the end. Must have used a wheelbarrow. Might even have some kind of protocol set up for visitors.

He had pulled himself into a sitting position by the sofa but was unarmed, still winded. "Forget somethin'?"

"Where are the keys, Danny?"

"Eat my dick."

"No thank you." I was dry all the way to my gut. I turned on his faucet and stuck my head under, rinsing off the stink, taking big mouthfuls, gargling, spitting. An eight-quart saucepan sat next to the sink and I was going to shower myself, but it was crusted with chili. I dried my face on a towel and asked him again. Same response.

"Fine." I took a bench from his table, grabbed the axe and knocked the legs off one end. "We did it your way. Now we'll do it mine." I grabbed him by the ankles and dragged him screaming to the bench, pulled his feet up on the high end, and duct-taped them in place. He tried to roll off and I rolled him back and punched him once to get his attention, then taped over his throat and around the bench. "Last chance, Danny Kent."

"Fuck you."

I'd only seen films, was never asked to do this in the field. But I was there, in the field, and it felt good. I took his beard. "What the hell is this anyway? Some ZZ-Top wannabe?" I pulled hard. "You *Talee-bhan*? *He*? *Nah*? *Hez bi-Islam*?" I felt some of the old energy come back. Bring it on. "*Mah kaw, Maut Mock, Kah wah*!"

I took a deep breath and closed my eyes; this could get so out of hand, and it occurred to me that I might like it that way— something big rising in my chest, so wonderful, monstrous and grand, I wanted to set it loose; I hadn't controlled anything in my world in months, and now I wanted to control everything, rip out his fucking heart and paint the walls with it. I bit my lip and leaned forward. It felt wonderful.

"Where are the keys?"

"You gonna kill me now?"

"You'll wish I had. Where are the fucking keys?"

"Up your asshole." He giggled and frothed a little blood.

"Have it your way." I filled the chili pot with cold water, scum still floating on the surface, dropped the towel over his face and poured. He screamed, gurgled, and I lay on his arms as he tried to flail, slowly emptying the pot. I wrapped the rest of the tape around him and refilled. I poured again and he gurgled, convulsed, tried to raise his head against the tape. We did this twice more, the water soaking the legs of my BDUs, spreading out over the worn, sandy floorboards, disappearing in the cracks. I sat cross-legged a few minutes and looked at him breathing, every gasp a triumph, then reached over and pulled the rag off. "The keys."

"Steps." He coughed. "Under the steps."

I retrieved the keys, came back, opened the Gerber and cut the tape around his neck, then his arms. I considered the feet but thought better. I sat by his head.

"What was it you were going to ask me to tell? What was so goddamn important, before you tore out my teeth?"

He groaned, pointed at the open cabin door.

"Outside?"

He wheezed and coughed. I held one of the inhalers to his lips. He inhaled deep, groaned again and raised his arm. "The sky. What are they?"

I went over and looked up. "The jet trails?"

He grinned, spat more blood. "Poison. What kind of poison?"

"They're just fuckin' jet trails, man. Water vapor."

- - -

Sun was setting over the mountains above his little part of the valley, the path back to the road almost erased by blue shadow. My face was swelling, my left eye starting to close, but I drove through the deep grass, made it to the hole in the fence before darkness fell. Once on the gravel, I accelerated, rolled down the windows and smelled mountain pines. About a mile down the road I hurled the AK pistons out the window, then the AR bolt. I considered the pistol but put it in the glove box. If I'd continued searching, I wonder now if I'd have found the decapitation photo. I could have spent another couple of hours there, but at that point just getting away was all-consuming. The place stunk.

So, the parents were drunks; not hard to justify with two kids like that. Or was it the other way around? Vasectomy at eighteen. What kind of parent allows something like that? What kind of brother lets that happen? Maybe it was a court order, statutory rape. They used to do that. He was only two years younger—not four. Must have flunked a couple of grades. If any kind of truth had passed between the two of us that afternoon, it was his little declaration, maybe one of the few truths he knew; he wasn't my uncle, and Andrew Kent wasn't my father. Not the kind of closure I'd set myself up to come home with.

My last little thread to the legendary Andy Kent was severed. Maybe Mom wasn't really Mom either. I wasn't related, at all, to people that no sane person would want to be related to anyway. I wasn't related to anybody. And Zilker thought this would be *therapeutic*. I began to laugh, laughing like a seizure, couldn't stop; fifteen years in the most hostile regions of the planet, looking for a fight, and I damn near get killed by one emphysematous old hermit in the woods, not far from Glacier National Park.

- - -

I'd filled the car the day before and had enough fuel to get back to Spokane. I drove through Whitefish, wanting to stop for water or a Mountain Dew, knowing I looked, smelled like a baboon, and fearing that I'd giggle again, do something absurd in public, draw attention. Too dirty to check into a motel, might even attract police, and so I watched the lights fade in the rearview and went on down Highway 93. I turned on the radio and the Stones' "Shattered" blasted forth, distorted, a favorite of Mrs. Dunham when she cleaned house, turned up loud as she ran the vacuum, and she'd voiceover—"rats in the *kitchen*, bedbugs, *upstairs*"—as she dragged the Hoover up to our rooms.

The cool air felt good on the back of my head and slowly the scald there dissipated. The adrenaline that circulates after battle crackled through me like electricity, through my fingers, my feet, the accelerator. There's an exhilaration after battle not because you've killed men, but because they were trying to kill you and failed; every faceoff is like being forced to leap from the roof of one skyscraper to another, fast, five, ten times in a row, so that when you're done you just want to wallow in life like a dog in stink, you're just so fucking blessed to be alive.

It was almost midnight when I passed an exit to Plains and, putting my hand in my pocket, remembered what became of Cheryl's card. Rain struck the windshield, one huge drop, then another, until it hammered the hood, the glass, the roof like a load of ball bearings. I pulled onto the shoulder and got out, face skyward, drenched, still laughing, pissed on by God himself and laughing, rain streaming down my arms, mouth filling with rain in the dark. Must have stood there until it blew over, until only silence and Montana wind surrounded me. Not another car passed.

Back in my seat again, pulling off my clothes, turning up the heat, I sensed loss, my mood plummeting, some vast deceleration of the soul. On through the night for hours, every drop of light leaked away by the time I pulled into a parking lot, reclined my seat and fell asleep. A while later I awakened briefly and chuckled again. In the right circumstances, waterboarding worked very well.

7

I woke up at 0534 hours, morning filtering through my lids and a visceral sense of increased traffic on the highway, the growl of the big rigs and the wake that followed them. Eyes open. Eyes left. Eyes right. Firenze Café, Florence, Montana, sunrise splintering off the sign. I climbed out of the car, stretched my legs, desperately needing to piss. Café was locked. I couldn't remember turning off the highway or parking the car. I stood by the front fender of my little Corolla, wishing for the moment I'd bought a pickup, and left a wet spot in the sand, brushing gravel over it with the side of my boot. Map flattened on the roof of the car, I had crossed I-90 last night without noticing and was now fifteen or twenty miles south of Missoula.

I drove north, turned west on 90, stopping at a rest area after a few miles. Crushed sacks from McDonald's emblazoned with tire tracks, used diapers, two tall Bud Ice cans sat by the curb. Four garbage barrels, none of them overloaded. Toilets had piss everywhere, flies patrolling the thick air. Magic-marker drawing, bottom half of a naked girl on the partition next to me, labeled *pusie*. Had to be sure we understood. Did look a little like a collapsed suspension bridge. A different hand had scratched *GARY'S* just before *pusie*. Graffiti in every toilet in the world, but nowhere as apolitical as home. Just the same old anatomy lesson—simple language and one-track minds. No wonder everybody thinks we're pigs.

I finished and washed my hands in the gritty white soap, trying to splash my face as well, but the faucet wouldn't stay on long enough. I didn't lock the car, not sure why not, but I remembered the Tokarev in the glove compartment and hurried out, hands and face still wet. Maybe the next toilet I visit, I'll scribble *DEAtH to grate sAtan Amerika* on the wall, some phony Arabic next to it, get the Homeland Security folks on point.

The pistol was still there. I locked the compartment. On patrol you never locked a vehicle— can't recall if there was a lock at all besides the chain and padlock we put on the steering at night in the pen. In the field one or two guys always stayed behind, ready to drive, one on point with the fifty. Push the big red button when you start it up again. Locking a vehicle when I leave still isn't a habit.

Backing out, more garbage blew across my windshield.

On returning from Germany I flew into Seattle, starved for grease and salt and fine-shaped asses on girls you could look at and talk to, any music you wanted, any book you wanted to read, or reread, any movie, anytime everything. I rented a car and almost immediately got lost, and did so every day, once making it as far as the Peace Arch at the border. I ran out of gas a couple of times. Got panicked once in a parking garage, took a ramp too quick and scraped a fender. Decided I got lost because I hadn't really been driving since I was a kid, in a big city ever, no horizon anywhere, so many fucking lights and signs and movement, bikes and cars and buildings and faces; sometimes you'd be stopped in the middle of all of it, unable to go forward or back or turn, wide-open and, always, shit-piles of stuff on the road that nobody seemed worried about. Nobody watching for the one guy with the phone who would detonate the charge. People with phones everywhere. Horns blowing behind you and you miss the fucking green. I'd get back to my room and close the blackouts, turn the air on high-cold and open a beer, stare at texture on the ceiling.

I managed to make it to and from South Center a couple of times, far more manageable. From the bluff up near the freeway you could scout the whole structure, the parking lot, some of the roof, the entrances, the exits. Always the exits. Found Half-Price Books and loaded so many in a box, almost everything I'd read in the past and lost or left behind, and countless others. I've saved almost every penny since I re-upped in '96, about 120 grand, and that month I spent 5,000 of it.

After a week of almost perpetual confusion, I settled into my room at the Capri Motor Hotel near the airport, kept curtains drawn, ordered in Chinese food, Mexican food, beer, even a hooker one night, nice girl with thick thighs, bright lips, clean teeth. She made small talk, rubbed my back, but nothing worked, couldn't do anything with her, limp, lost, unable to turn off my mind for a second. I closed my eyes and wondered if she was going to run a razor across my throat as soon as I fell asleep, all of her kindness some kind of polished act. Begged her to sleep with me anyway. She stayed because she couldn't get another assignment so late, but she was gone by 0500.

I started wondering if there was any place I belonged, started to think I was like the ANA guys, who could never really go home. No disability or insurance for them and, for a lot of them, once they left their village they were *persona non grata*, could never go back. Lot of gay guys in the ANA as well. No gay district to hang out in, stoneable offense if the Taliban got ahold of you. So they'd go in the ANA, probably because it was the only place to meet other gays, knowing they were going to die there.

One morning I just woke up, packed all my gear, got a taxi down to the bus station and came to Spokane, like a light clicked on. Original notion was to go back to Colville, but I hesitated, like you might at the door of a girl you haven't seen in a long time, uncertain if you should knock. Maybe I thought I *was* going to meet girls, girls I knew in school, girls I'd thought about for a decade or more, who hadn't changed at all, and the world was going to be there just like I'd left it. But I already knew it wasn't, from my brief visit in the winter so many years prior, and in the end I settled in Spokane Valley. After I was discharged from the VA I stopped buying beer.

Climbing higher in the mountains, still westbound on I-90, I kept the Corolla at about sixty, feeling like I might have abused her the night before, terrified her into thinking me a maniac at the wheel as she listened to my every word, every laugh, becoming distracted and ultimately lost.

The cut on my arm was outlined by an inch of redness, throbbing with heat, getting infected. Hard to know what Danny used that knife for, what dried corruption was layered on the blade. Might have used it to gut a skunk or murder people—who knows what I might find with a real recon: meter men, hunters, hikers, Boy Scouts, Mormons and their bicycles a foot or two beneath that uneven turf. I pictured him puffing away, shovel in hand, body parts in the wheelbarrow, stopping to use his inhaler every once in a while. Occasionally he looks up at the jet trails suspiciously, and reassures himself he's done a good deed, God's work.

Shithouse rat. I hadn't used that term very often, usually heard other guys say it, but now I understood it in a personal way I could taste. Danny was crazy, paranoid with a complexity no one could rehabilitate, and I wondered if it took a lifetime to get him there, or if the voices came while he was in high school or working at one of those numerous jobs he'd written to his aunt about, scampering around a half-framed house, hammer in hand, talking to himself, kneeling to pray at high noon while his co-workers sat on the front seats of pickups, doors open, eating their KFC and laughing at him.

I downshifted coming up on Lookout Pass, a long column of big rigs in the right lane, flashers on, crawling in low gear; one of them crawling a little faster had decided to pass. Head of the column was a fuel truck. I let off the accelerator and waited for the streak of blue smoke to dart from the trees, burst the side of the tank, waited to feel the heat as I got roasted with thirty other guys. But I'm not sure anybody sees the rocket that kills them, except Marsden, and I thought of the fins sticking out of him, red running out of the new mouth, lips, punched into his liver.

He must have known that his ass was gone.

Such a trite way to put it: ass gone. We say something, an expedient summary of what we really mean but won't talk about. Did Marsden know at that moment that he was going to be put in a body bag an hour later, that he'd never get married or see his hometown again, or drink a beer or love a girl or have a kid, that the numbing cold coming over him wasn't the IV, the sleepiness wasn't the morphine, but all of his blood abandoning him into the sand?

The traffic thinned at the peak and we all began the long dive into Idaho. I wondered how long it took Danny Kent to untape his ankles. I left the door open and I felt bad. Something big might have wandered in and eaten him alive, but he was so fixated on looking at the sky. Maybe he had some other equally crazy friend, one of the "others" he spoke of, and they'd drop by for a nice pipe of meth and find him there. And I thought of his face when I pulled the wet rag away, every facial muscle trembling, and what I'd read about the godawful dread one could cause with such a simple procedure, leaving a prisoner in every other way unmarked.

I was surprised that I did it, that it came so easily, that I might have actually enjoyed it, and I looked at my arm, felt my face and remembered it was not an easy day. *I got my car keys back and didn't have to kill anybody, thank you.* I thought about Cheryl, if I would ever see her confident face again, a face that might have made the sun come up or settled a war, and how I lost her card, and I'm not sure any amount of torture I could have inflicted on Danny would avenge that act.

- - -

It was quiet at the apartment, no kid sounds or Jennifer's voice through the wall, unusual on a Sunday. How could I describe to her what I went through with my "Uncle Danny"? Next to him she was a paragon of rational thought.

I showered until the water ran cold, used my back brush everywhere, over the painful, swollen laceration on my arm, even brushed my face. If it fit in my mouth I would have scrubbed my tongue.

Drying off, wrapped in a towel, I fell asleep on my futon with afternoon sun flooding the kitchen. Dreams came and went, but I didn't awaken until the next morning, and when I did I was drenched and shivering.

I made a double cup of instant coffee, sat at the kitchen table with a blanket around me and opened the last three letters. I flattened the pages, then looked at the envelopes again. No *Free* in the corner. Some brittle, wavy distortion in the paper, as if they'd been wet at one point. I held the first page in the light.

Donna,

Was great seeing you, and my oh my your grown up. Surprized the shit out of me at Club North. Yes I want to see you again. What boy wouldn't? (after _that_ weekend!)

Yes, Ive seen "HIM" here. A couple of times when I was in Long Bien. Had a bunch of cameras and meters and shit around his neck, looked more like some body from a magazine than a soldier. Click click click like a jap tourist. Pictures for Stars & Stripes or some such bullshit. Tried to act like he knew me, like we were good buds from way back. Asked what I was going to do when we got back to the 'real' world. I said, hey asshole, this IS the real world. Not sure he's going to live through this, head up his ass in all kinds of ideas. You were right in changing your priorities.

War can be hell, but mostly just reshuffling the deck, you know? War can be OPPORTUNITY. More about that later. I'm going to send you some stuff. Don't open till I get home, and don't show it to anybody.

Will be in country for a couple of months, way in country. See you, I hope, in Seattle, somewhere around Christmas? Things are winding down over here, gotta get what I can.

Andy

It took me at least thirty minutes to soak up the idea. "Like a Jap tourist." My dad was that man. And this was a different man, Andy Kent. Andy Kent, who had a vasectomy two years before I was born. I sat there until my arm ached, and I realized it had swollen as if a large green bean were sewn beneath the skin, and I was sweating again. I picked up the two remaining letters and my still packed suitcase.

— — —

I vomited in the VA emergency room lobby. They put an IV in my arm and ran in a bag of antibiotics, some other drugs, and drew enough blood, I estimated, to transfuse another vet.

Doctor was an older guy, said he'd been a corpsman. "Why'd you let this thing get so bad?" He cleared some lidocaine from a syringe and started stinging his way around the wound. "Got yourself a fine little abscess here."

"Only been a couple of days."

He cut an opening near my elbow and two tablespoons of rotten yellow curd ran out, smelling like decayed meat. He started pressing a strip of fabric into the opening. "This is a packing," he said. "Stays in until this is almost healed." He cut the end off, leaving a little tail sticking out. "Have your wife or girlfriend, buddy, pull out about an inch each day."

"I live by myself."

"You go to Afghanistan by yourself?"

"What do you think?"

"Folks? Family?"

I shook my head.

He wrapped Kerlix around my arm. "People live longer with a partner."

After a couple of hours I felt better, but the doctor said I should be admitted, stay for a few days of IV antibiotics. I refused and thanked them anyway. They asked me to sign a paper saying that I might lose my arm or die if I didn't go in the hospital but sent me off with a grenade-sized bottle of antibiotics, some hydrocodone, and a number to call if I got worse.

When I reached the interstate I turned into the sunset and headed back to the Yakima valley, driven to find Richard Nelson, or whatever remained of his family.

8

Four Nelsons were listed: two in Sunnyside, one in Zillah, one in Grandview. The first address was a condominium. An accommodating fellow of about sixty with a ruddy face and silver moustache answered the door. He had only recently moved there from Fresno to be the hospital administrator. The second address was a few rows over in the same trailer park where I'd found Millie Kent. No cars were in the driveway and I sat there for ten minutes or more, wondering what I wanted to ask, who would know or care about two kids' infatuation thirty-eight years past. I was working a hunch, like they say in detective novels. A hunch that no one else would likely understand and might be considered invasive. We have satellites that can pass over your house twenty miles up, read the license plate of your car, while everybody is trying to protect the privacy of shit no one cares about. It's as if people, disempowered from the real grand scheme, find something they can be in charge of and obsess over it.

Not long after I'd landed in Bagram, I took a picture of an Afghan girl. Just a girl sitting outside of a school. Everyone was fascinated at the time with the photo of a green-eyed girl on

National Geographic, and I guess I was pretending to be a photo journalist. Her brother—or father, couldn't really tell—went ballistic. At one point he started to pull a pistol and everybody took him down, cuffed him. The captain took my little Canon and held it next to his face and deleted the picture. He seemed to relax at that. We let him go and he continued to yammer at me in Pashtu, pointing, spitting. The girl had a skateboard, but I wasn't allowed to take her picture. Go figure.

I got out of the Corolla and went to the door. No one answered. Shielding my eyes at the window I saw most of the front room, outlines in the carpet where furniture had been moved away. Only a blue velour recliner remained.

I drove back into town, past the Sunrise Convalescent Center, where an odd stab of intuition, a wild whisper, took my ear and I U-turned. At the reception desk I asked to see Mrs. Palmer.

The silver-haired receptionist fumbled about, said she didn't know the residents yet, she was new there, when an aide, a tall girl of about twenty, came through the locked double doors.

"Mindy? Can you take this nice gentleman to see Mrs. Palmer?"

The girl regarded me uncertainly, then motioned me to follow her back the way she had come, and the doors clicked behind us.

"You're the first visitor she's ever had. I think."

She spoke forward, ahead of me. She turned and simultaneously I noticed how breathlessly pretty the girl was, even the tiny gold ring in her eyebrow, and how foul the air hung in the corridor, thick with fresh feces and old urine. She stopped at a doorway and looked in.

"I think she needs to be changed." And she walked off. As an afterthought she called back to me, "You know she don't talk."

I entered the room, a chrome-railed hospital bed set low to the floor, the frail sawbuck, rawboned outline of a human, turned, curled like a fetus toward the window. I stepped around the bed until I cast a shadow over the hollow face, the lenses of her eyes opaque, incapable of focus, unable to reflect light, joy.

I fingered her wrist band. In large characters after her name, *03/15/32:DNR*.

"Cora Palmer?"

No response.

I reached down gently, found her thready little trapezius, and gave it a firm pinch.

Nothing. I don't even think she gathered anything deeper than her already agonal breaths. I stepped back.

On the wall opposite the foot of the bed, a cheaply-framed, color-faded portrait of my mother, age eighteen, wearing a cap and gown. Brown dust on the windowsill. Dead flies in the track of the window, small cobwebs. A courtyard was beyond the window, untended, a metal bench and patio table covered in bird excrement. Dead flowers, a few wild thistles, a dying tree stood motionless in the heat.

I had the snapshot of my mother on the pier in Seattle, easy enough to compare to the graduation picture should anyone query my business there, but in the following minutes no one came to the room at all. After a while, I walked back up the hall. Mindy spotted me from another patient's room and key-carded me out. I felt dizzy, hungry for fresh air as I got into the Corolla. The creature I'd just seen was only seventy-six but looked to be ninety. I wondered if life would end that way for me, feeling like I'd opened a grave. She was my grandmother, I presumed, unless another web of lies lurked in my mother's family tree as well.

\- - -

I drove north on Washout Road, then west for twenty minutes of rise and fall without passing anyone, just the race of hops and grapes, then orchards, then fields of unknown short green rows. A right turn on Beam Road, another two miles and a right on Houghton Road, easily 500 feet above the valley floor, the fields low and thick with alfalfa. I slowed and stopped at the numbered, unnamed box and turned up the gravel drive, apprehensive, wondering if I'd run into Danny again, or somebody like him.

Dust boiled up behind my car and blew past my window as I slowed to a stop and killed the engine. A meadowlark sang in the stifling silence of midday. A large, brick-red barn stood askew, door half open, empty inside. I stepped out and walked a few yards, stopping at a set of concrete steps that rose through the weeds a few tiers, leading to a large, charred rectangle, the outline of a footing, a collapsed fireplace, the melted, rusted shell of a water heater. About thirty feet by forty, the center was punctuated here and there with new weeds rising through the ash. On each side of the steps, a massive tangle of white roses struggled into the air, phosphorescent in the sun.

I leaned on the hood of the car for a few minutes, defeated, arm throbbing, pulse pounding, perspiration running from my scalp, burning my eyes. Every positive outcome I had envisioned ended in this dirty, dusty, hopeless dead end. I swiveled into the driver's seat and a head rush of heat.

At the corner about a half mile away sat a double-wide, a manicured lawn, and a circular, red cinder driveway, a greenhouse far in the backyard abutting some ranch fencing. I turned in and stopped. They would know something. Neighbors know everything. Maybe they would have water. I needed to see living people.

An air conditioner hummed from a curtained window. A plywood ramp covered with green Astroturf led to the front door. I knocked, twice. I knocked again. Nothing. I was about to turn away when the door rattled and an ancient man folded into a wheelchair rolled backwards, pulling it open. His skeletal face rose and his eyes grew large, his jaw fell. He seemed to gather his breath; then, a long, pathetic wail, pointing at me and slamming his contracted arm into the door, looking over his shoulder, taking a breath only to wail again.

"I'm sorry," I said. "I've got the wrong house. I'm really sorry." And I backed away, turning halfway down the ramp to run to the car. When I looked up he had rolled his chair almost into the glass, still waving his good hand and crying out, the aluminum shaking as he kicked at the bottom panel. I started the engine and rolled around the circular drive. A gaunt, silver-haired woman dashed across my path, waving her arms, uncanny energy in a stiff gray dress. I turned slightly to go around her, and she stepped into my way again, then patted the hood of the car like you'd pat a horse, coming around to the window.

"I'm sorry," I repeated. "I've come to the wrong house." I glanced beyond her at the screen door. "I didn't mean to upset anyone."

She said nothing for a moment, swaying slightly, dissecting every curve of my face for some sort of authenticity. "You're at the right house. Come in. Please come in."

I turned off my engine and sat there a moment. Her expression resolute, every fold and fissure in her face like a well-oiled old boot.

"Please," she said. "You don't look well." She touched my cheek.

I followed her up the ramp to the screen door. The old man had vanished. She directed me into the semi-dark of the living room, where I collapsed onto a sofa.

"Larry," she called. "Larry, come out here. We have a visitor." She wandered to the bright side of the house and I heard ice cubes drop in a glass. She returned with a glass of water. "I think he went into the bathroom. He needs to come out and get control of himself. Poor dear." She pushed an ottoman over to my feet.

"Thank you." I drank my water. "I really should be going. I only stopped because I thought you might know something about the burned house. Up on the bluff."

"I can tell you a lot. But it's not for sale, if that's your reason for coming." But she looked at me as if she already knew why I was there. "What's your name?"

I told her, and her sense of familiarity faded. A door down the hall squeaked.

"I'm looking for a man named Richard Nelson. He had a friend in high school. Donna Palmer."

"Well, my name is *Rita* Nelson." She stepped in the dining room momentarily and returned with a gilded frame. "This Richard Nelson?"

The man was in uniform, the same distant pose that Andy Kent had assumed. I ran my fingers along the frame, fingertips numb. He looked like me.

"And who is Donna Palmer to you?" Her voice came from far above me.

"She was my mother."

The woman sat next to me, turning my face gently away from the photograph I still held. "Then you are probably"—she halted, closing her eyes briefly—"our grandson."

I looked back at the photo again. Richard Nelson looked very different from the slouching, long-haired kid I'd seen sitting next to Mom in the yearbook. We both sat in silence until something brushed my ankle, the foot platform of a wheelchair. The old man had wheeled himself back in without my noticing and now sat silent, like someone in a prayer circle.

"This isn't our Richard, dear," she took his hand. "It's his boy. Our grandchild." The old man was weeping.

I felt trapped, like an imposter who had no business eliciting so much sorrow, or elation. I had terrified the old man—my grandfather, I suppose—and was now going to be subject to some unearned coronation. I didn't know what to say. "Where is he now?"

She took the photo and hugged it against her torso. "He's dead. Two years." She rose and went into the dining room where she turned on a light, and I followed. An arrangement of photos hung on the wall above a marble-topped buffet that, equally adorned, took on the appearance of an altar. She opened the blinds across the table and flooded it with afternoon sun.

"He died of lymphoma. Agent Orange, you know. He was fifty-one." The frames spread like a timeline across the wall. In one photo he held a woman close to his face, her white lace enveloping them both, a portrait of two souls. She saw me studying it.

"That was Karla. Richard was thirty. She was a little older, couldn't have children." She took the photo down and turned it over, as if it might explain something. "She was very good to him, though."

"Have any picture from when he married my Mom?"

She didn't answer, shook her head.

"He threw them away?"

Searching my face she said, "They never—" She shook her head once more. "They never married."

I was dumbstruck. "My big day for surprises."

"He asked her and she said yes, they made announcements and then she just kept putting it off, over and over." She sat in one of the dining room chairs and motioned for me to do the same, but I kept standing.

"Finally, Richard lost his leave once, and she acted like it was his fault. She kept the ring but stopped calling here after that. Then somebody saw them in Seattle, she and the Kent boy." She was still shaking her head, as if she'd never come to grips with it herself. "He's not your father, you know. Andy Kent. I hope you realize that."

All too well. It was a big bundle of loose tarp in the windstorm of my head and I struggled to push it all out of the way. We both stared at the photos on the wall awkwardly. I turned finally to a square one I recognized, grainy in enlargement. "I have this picture. Mom saved it."

"Richard and Vicky," she smiled.

"But who was Vicky?"

"The car, silly boy. A Crown Victoria. Larry's first car." She nodded toward the old man.

The old man managed to enunciate, "Fifty-six."

"Ricky saved it from the junkyard, restored every screw and bolt on it."

She turned back into the living room, opening one blind after another, great shafts of sun filling the little house. I followed her down a hallway and she stopped and turned, flipping on a light. A photograph hung on the wall, sixteen by twenty at least, a mural of mountain-scape rising from a bed of clouds, a few wisps in the stratosphere illuminated by moonlight.

"He took that on the way up to Ellensburg. Nighttime. Time exposure. He won a prize for that." She showed me another framed photo in a bedroom, seemingly below the surface of a lake, a fish in shadows of grass. Another showed weary men swaddled against the pouring rain, a city street, gray and black and white. "That one"—she touched the glass with her nail—"was in *Seattle Magazine*."

"So, he was a photographer even after the Army," I said.

"And before. Sounds like you already know a little bit about him."

"I knew some. Just didn't know he was my father."

"He and Karla gave a lot to the Boys and Girls Club, and he took photographs every year at the proms for just the cost of his film. Every kid in the school knew him. I think he was trying to compensate for not having children of his own."

— — —

We ate mostly in silence, islands of conversation popping up every few minutes. I told them about my time in the Army, leaving out my brief marriage, the time in Kosovo, the bag of medication in my backpack. Larry, I realized, was not just staring at me, but my eye, specifically. "The letters that he sent to Mom. He signed them with the letter *A,* just an initial."

Larry and Rita exchanged glances. She smiled. "There was a singer back then, before then, really. Ricky Nelson." She sighed. "Very *un-cool*. It turned into a joke at school, so after Richard was twelve or so, he insisted we call him by his middle name, Aaron." She paled. "You're bleeding."

I looked down and the bandage had oozed through my shirt. "A little misunderstanding," I said. "I wandered on to the property of a guy up in Whitefish, thought he was my uncle." And then I explained the Kents.

"They weren't good boys. Something always in the paper, police reports you know." She stood, went down the hall, returned from the bathroom a moment later with scissors and a roll of gauze.

"Your father was a good boy. Helped his father. That was the house he grew up in, the one that burned." She tied a little knot, then rolled my sleeve down but frowned at her work. "We were farmers. When Larry hurt his back, we leased the land and bought an antique mall downtown." She held a bowl of green beans out to me and I shook my head. "When Richard died, well, Larry had a stroke, and we moved down here. Rented the old house and damned if they didn't burn it down the first year."

I learned my father had been a photographer, first for a newspaper, and later he had a studio. "Army gave him a skill," I said. "Not sure what I've learned that I can put to use here."

"It wasn't easy for him. He cried a lot when he came back, lived with us. We thought it was about Donna at first, but then he'd wake up, say something was dead in the barn. Could smell it, he said. Was always looking for a dead lamb, saying we'd missed it." She covered her face with her napkin. "It turned out his last position with the Army was in Saigon, where they put the bodies in caskets to go home, what was left of them. Richard had to photograph each and every one." She pushed her chair back. "Excuse me." She made a small cry and went to the kitchen. When she came back she had regained her composure.

"You're very welcome to stay here. It's late." She set a pie on the table. "So what do you think you'll go into, now that you're out? What skill did you learn?"

I sat staring at my pie for a painful period of time.

"Robert?"

They were both looking at me, so honestly, so paternal. They really wanted to know and didn't deserve my cynicism. I could turn another man's head into aerosol at 800 yards. I really could. Not everybody can do that, half a fucking mile away, not like in the movies. You have to lead a man, estimate his speed, if he's walking or running, so his head meets the bullet. I almost whispered this and glanced at each of them to be certain I hadn't said it loud enough, but their faces were still full of inquiry.

"You don't have to tell us right now." Rita reached over and squeezed my hand. "Maybe you don't know yet."

"I'm not sure," I said. "I'm not sure what I'm going to be good at. I'm not even sure who I am anymore." I pushed my chair back, stood, walked over to the Buffet of Ricky. "Your son's boy, I guess. Sounds like he was a great guy. But I grew up thinking

I had to be some kind of damned warrior, and now I'm not sure I even liked what I did, and I can't do it anymore anyway, and what—how—would I be different?" I flopped in a wing chair at the corner of the dining room. Larry had backed his wheelchair so he could see me; he was alarmed, afraid perhaps. Rita sat imperturbable on the far side of the table.

"We were farmers," she said. "We farmed until Larry couldn't anymore, but we still get up every morning at four, and I find him sitting out here in the kitchen, listening to that little radio, to the farm reports. It just became part of us." She went to the kitchen, came back with a coffee pot and three heavy white cups. "Care for some?"

I shook my head.

"When your father came back from Vietnam, he wasn't a farmer anymore. He was a photographer. He'd taken a lot of awful photographs and I suppose that was stuck inside his head, but through the years he took a look of beautiful pictures as well." She looked down at her pie and seemed surprised that she hadn't finished. She picked up her fork. "Perhaps, in the end"— she took a bite—"who you are depends on what you've done the most of. It becomes part of you."

I resumed my seat at the table and realized it would be rude if I didn't eat her pie, which looked like blueberry, and had clearly been homemade. Larry relaxed and sipped his coffee.

We made more small talk; they showed me Dad's cameras, all Nikons, heavily worn, dented, substantial in the hand. We talked about how hardly anyone processed film anymore, and the coming of computers, and cell phones, and how his time in Vietnam might have been different if they could have emailed or talked every day. He kept a .45 in his camera bag wherever he went, and it bothered Karla. He was equally fond of an angle-head flashlight that he brought back from the war, now wedged in the cushion of Larry's wheelchair. I was in the museum of Ricky Aaron Nelson and hadn't even bought a ticket, like a ragged straggler stumbling into a primitive valley and being made king because the locals think my face looks like some ancient carving on a temple.

On the way back to the dining room she pressed one of Nikons into my hands. "He'd want you to have it," she said.

"I can't take this." I tried to hand it back.

"And where will it end up when we are gone?" She set it by my chair.

I sat alone with Larry at the table and tried to have a conversation while Rita made a bed on the couch. He could erupt one-word answers and he retrieved a satin box from the buffet. Dad got a Purple Heart for some sort of head injury, but Larry couldn't elaborate how or when. When I told him I had one of those too he nodded and hummed approvingly and shook my hand.

"Whatever you become," she added, "you'll always be our grandson."

Larry tried to smile, but his paralysis turned it into a leer. As sincere as I thought they both were, I felt like I did when I strayed into an evangelical church in Columbus, and everyone laid hands on me and tried to make me feel saved, and all it did was make me feel horribly alone.

■ ■ ■

By 2200 the house was dark, just a few slits of light through the curtains from the security light over the driveway. I slept for about ninety minutes and woke up thinking about Jennifer and tried to imagine where all of her hostility came from, she who had lived a pretty uninterrupted life, so far as I knew. How could she judge what I'd done, not having been there? How could anyone but one of my platoon, or anyone who has spent almost six years in a place where anyone can put a bullet in your face? Even a child, even a dead, inanimate thing, a rotting dog carcass, could explode and mix parts of a man in the air with shreds of decay so you didn't know what you were putting in the body bag, soldier or animal, all the time breathing molecules of both. How could I tell her about that? *I'll try*, I thought. *Once more.* Even pretend to smoke some of her pot.

All kinds of pictures came back. Watching our six. People

count on you to watch their six. I thought about Marsden. I thought about the two insurgents I'd shot. I saw them go down. I shot them. I fucking shot them. Just thirty yards away. Less. I liked to change magazines before I was empty. I left one in the chamber, dropped the clip and put another twenty beneath it, and in that time one of those two sat up, squeezed the trigger on an RPG. I took him down again, the back of his head coming off, but by that time a rocket was stuck in Marsden, and him looking so surprised. If I'd just kept my point of aim, just a couple seconds more, that motherfucker would have popped up and I would have nailed him. Marsden would have lived, but instead he was looking at me, *me*, looking shocked.

— — —

They had a grandfather clock that chimed every thirty minutes, and at 0300 I realized I wasn't going back to sleep, and thought about taking an extra pill, but then I'd be too stupid to talk when they got up in another hour or so. When I rolled onto my left a dull ache arose in my left calf, and reaching down I felt a soft swelling the size of a pea. I slipped my shoes on, scribbled a quick note and left it by the radio, said I would return when I'd figured some things out, thanked them for their hospitality and understanding, and left my apartment address in Spokane. I took the camera, pushed the lock button in on the front door as I left, and drove off slowly in the half-moon shadows without turning on my lights.

And I wondered, driving that descent into the valley, the town lights feeble on the horizon, what my father felt driving that same asphalt, what song was playing on the radio, what excitement might have blessed his night, or what worried him, about finishing high school, about joining the Army, or if he was drafted, and the hopes he'd had with Donna, what plans he'd made that were forever derailed by that time.

I pulled over and I cried. For that loss, what he never knew, the good parts of life that were taken from him. For the fact that we never met, even though I could have driven down here from

Fort Lewis a dozen times in those years he was still alive. For my own lifetime I could never tell him about, that our paths never intersected.

By 0500 I was headed north on 395. I snapped my head up, having drifted off, then pinched myself, rolled the window down, bounced in the seat every couple of seconds to stay awake. I pulled into a rest area surrounded by scrub sage and a handful of stunted locust trees for shade. The same litter scattered on the asphalt, like I'd seen in Montana but not as much; my last thought was that maybe the wind here was stronger.

When I woke up about eight, the parking lot was full of cars; a blue crew-cab Chevy pickup with extremely loud door hinges was disembarking a family by my open window. Next to me on the seat, the Nikon, staring at the dash like some little orphaned animal I'd adopted and didn't know how to feed. I took an antibiotic and washed it down at the drinking fountain. I felt good, relatively, and a long list of tasks seemed to grow before me as I rolled down the onramp onto the highway.

I took the Sprague exit and cruised along looking for a nursery, settling on the garden department of Lowe's, where, after coming to grips with my complete ignorance of horticulture, I let a skinny pony-tailed guy sell me a sack of potting soil, a crepe myrtle, and a yellow-and-red-striped pot to replant it in. "Girls like these," he said.

I set the plant in my kitchen sink and watered it, then got in the shower. Afterward, I replanted it in the striped pot, pressing my fingers in the soft soil while I was drying off, walking around my apartment naked, feeling primal. "Back to the earth," I said under my breath. A yellow bruise was present where I'd felt the pea on my leg. My arm was healing, dry and flat. Everything was healing. I skipped the underwear and pulled on some clean BDUs, shirt open.

- - -

I knocked on Jennifer's door and clumsy footsteps sounded within. A heavy Hispanic guy answered and pushed a trashcan into the hall. "Can I help you?"

"Is Jennifer here?"

"Sorry. She doesn't live here anymore. We're just moving in."

"I'm Robert." I nodded my head toward my apartment. "Next door."

"I'm Ramon."

He offered a hand and I shook it. A slighter man approached him from behind.

"This is Raul." Raul put an arm around Ramon's waist. "Yeah. She moved out, we guess. Owed a couple of months and the manager said if we cleaned it up we could have half a month free."

Raul held the portfolio in his free hand.

"Those were hers," I said. "Her drawings."

He looked down like he'd forgotten he had them. "We found them. Under the bed."

"Yeah. The bed." I remembered the bed.

"You want them?" He held them forward through the door.

"Yeah. That'd be great." I took them with my free hand. "Thank you."

He glanced at my pot. "That a crepe myrtle?"

"Yeah."

"Oh, I just adore those."

"You want it?"

He looked up at Ramon, who said, "It's up to you."

I held it out. "Think of it as a housewarming present."

I could have kept the plant, but it would have died on my balcony after I forgot to water it. I'm not a farmer.

I sat on one of the kitchen chairs and looked around my apartment for a long time, feeling like it wasn't really a home, just a gathering of my stuff behind a secure door. A storage container that I could sleep in. I hadn't put anything on the walls. I opened Jennifer's portfolio and held up one picture, and then another, but they seemed just as out of place as my bookcase, my calendar from the VA, my pile of half-empty duffels in the hall, and someone else's thirty-five-year-old love letters spread out across the table. Just as out of place as me. I opened the last letter and flattened it.

Sorry Baby—

Seattle ain't gonna happen. I've got a good deal here, way too good to let go of right this minute, but I'll be in country longer. Made E-5 last week, but part of LRRP now, and fighting the war on my terms, and takin' care of business when I come across it. More packages coming your way. Just put them in the bottom of your freezer. Please do not open, and do not discuss with your friends.

   We'll live good. Top floor at the Sands. Can't wait much longer to have you again, see you dressed up, see you naked. In this day and age a man has to have variety, and I got all that with you. Just have to pull off this little mission I designed for myself. And US.

   See you (ALL of you) in May.

Love Andy

What a fuckhead. So he'd been a LuRP. Fit him well. Should have taken his brother with him. Tough guys, but more than one story of craziness in the jungle. What was he sending her? *Jesus H. Christ. Heroin. Had to be.* No cocaine in Southeast Asia. Marijuana would be too big. Had to be heroin. Lot of guys doing that, a lot of guys getting caught, back in Vietnam.

I slouched in my chair, turned the envelope over and over in my fingers, then stopped. Pale wavy ink, a cancellation pale as a watermark, approached the corner but ended. The stamp had been steamed off. I picked up the previous letter and its stamp had been steamed off as well.

I grabbed the coaster from the Acorn and turned it over, picked up my cell and punched in the number.

"Is Kaye there?"

"Can I ask who's calling?" It was Mrs. Dunham, and her voice didn't sound any different than it had when I was fifteen, and I soaked it in for a second or two.

"Robby, ma'am."

"Robby Kent? I was hoping you'd call. You know Kaye was so excited when we got home that morning!"

Her voice waltzed some kind of joy, turbulent with questions, and I answered everything I could and told her I was fine and no, my injuries were nothing, and it was good to be back and no I didn't have a job, but I was getting a pretty good compensation and I was going to wait and can I please talk to Kaye, right now?

She hesitated. "She's not living here anymore, Robert. Moved out a week ago, into a cabin with Don Boffman, north of Kettle Falls." Another pause. "I'm sorry."

Older guy, electrician. She was real happy. I said I was happy for her. The conversation droned on for a few more minutes and I promised I'd come see them, and I intended to. I wanted to see Mr. Dunham again. Thank him. Not sure I ever did when I lived there. I wanted to see Mrs. Dunham again as well.

I closed the phone, tumbling the coaster with my other hand when it occurred to me I could try to email Kaye. A few minutes later I had set up an account, the edges of the screen filled with pictures, some weather girl whose dress fell off, some lawsuit about a drug, and strawberry growers are *furious* after the president said he liked chocolate ice cream. Why should I care? Pushing my buttons. Pushing buttons has become the national fucking pastime. I opened a new message and zoned it all out.

> KAYE—,JUST TALKED TO YOUR MOM, AND I'M REAL happy that you're
> happy. Sorry I dont type well, U R my first e-mail in years. You remember those letters
> that were in my suitcase? DID U soak some stamps off? REAL REAL important
> if you did. WHERE WERE THEY FROM/ ? Robby.

I watched my screen expectantly for about three minutes before it dawned on me that her computer probably didn't ring like a phone, and I'd just have to wait until she saw it.

I went out, bought some groceries, put some gas in the car. *Jennifer might swing by*, I thought, *to leave a note with her new address, or say goodbye*; I picked up a six-pack of Coors sixteen-ouncers. When I returned, kayegirl27 had answered.

> Robby,
> Thank you I'm very happy, I think. Janelle and Zach are happy, and they say Hi.
> I knew just where to look for those stamps, at the very back of my album. I had a picture of you in 11th grade there too. Just had two stamps—1 from Vietnam, really big, has a leopard on it. And another smaller one that has a sword stuck through a globe, says 'Republique Khmere.' Not sure where it was from. I'll send them to you, since they were never really mine. Am going to keep the picture.
> Love, K.

The very last letter had carried the smaller stamp. Khmere. Cambodia, last place he mailed anything from. Maybe that was where the head picture came from. Not sure why a man would want to send such a picture to the woman he cared about; even a sociopath like Andy would know that was a stupid move. Maybe someone added it to the envelope, personal little gag.

I liked looking at *Love, K.* I didn't belong with her, but it was sort of flattering. I thought a long time about deleting her letter, but in the end kept it. Seems weird to me that we can just wipe out the thoughts people send us so easily. On my kitchen table sat a whole stack of thoughts from 1971, all of them unaltered from the time the ink hit the page.

The post-it note Zilker gave me was stuck below the keyboard. *Together We Served.* Garcia was the only guy still there at the end. Lori. We called him Lori. I Googled him and opened the TWS page. Great picture, Purple Heart, and—the fuck—he was dead. Two months ago. Memorials could be sent to Mountainair People's Clinic, Mountainair, NM.

Looked up the clinic, phoned them. Nice people. Said he'd had an accident with a gun, gave me his wife's number. I sat and drew circles around her number till the pen tore through the paper. *Accident. With a gun.* He didn't have any fucking accident. I couldn't fucking believe it. I phoned; the number rang, six, seven times.

A kid answered.

I remembered pictures of his kids. Couldn't remember what they looked like. "Is your dad there?"

"I . . . I better let you talk to my mom."

Fuck. More silence. Some muffled conversation, an adult, maybe in another room.

"She doesn't want to talk to anybody right now. Are you the realtor?"

Are they selling the house? She sounded like a young teen. "No," I said. "I served with your dad in Afghanistan."

"Dad's dead. She doesn't want to talk to anybody from the Army. Says you guys screwed up his head."

"I'm sorry." The line went dead.

My screen margins were alive with refinance ads, weight loss gimmicks, single girls looking for a date, all of them with lots of cleavage, looking like models or weather girls, girls in magazines, girls that littered the sidewalk in Vegas. It was a scam, sure as hell, like the hawkers and pimps in every city anywhere I'd ever been a soldier, preying on the lonely. Nobody ever met anybody through a little, flat, glass-and-plastic device full of particles of light, and the longer I sat and stared at it, the more angry, the more cheated I started to feel, that the world had come down to this, one fucking sales pitch after another, while I was busy trying to stay alive for fifteen years, ostensibly trying to make the planet safer for people who didn't know how fucking tenuous it all was. And now Garcia's family hated me and everybody like me.

I opened one of the beers and sat at the kitchen table looking over the parking lot, slowly shredding the letter from Cambodia into little fragments. When the first beer was gone I opened a second, and when it was gone I threw my bag in the car and drove to the interstate.

I wanted to eviscerate Andy Kent, tie him down and carve through his neck, disembowel him while he watched, for merely existing, ruining my parents' marriage, but some Cambodian had probably availed himself of that privilege decades ago. I would go see Danny Kent instead, and we would communicate like nothing he'd ever encountered. I just got angrier and angrier—at my drunk mother, at the war that doused my father with Agent Orange, the recruiter who tricked me into pissing away fifteen years, the hajji who killed Marsden. Angry at Zilker for not acknowledging this awful waste of a life, angry at the wheel in my hand, the glass of the windshield, angry at the sky, raging against the river of chaos that fucked so ceaselessly with my life. Angry at Garcia for fucking giving up. I got him through two tours; he got me through, we got each other through, and he comes back and offs himself. *Fuck. Accident with a gun my ass.* Meticulous guy, cleaned his Beretta like he was doing surgery.

The beers sat in a cooler on the seat. By the time I reached the Montana border all four cans lay folded on the passenger floor. I stopped at a Chevron, took a piss, bought a forty-ounce Mickey's and a bag of pork skins. I was still thirsty. Around sunset I rolled into Plains.

My plan was simple—drunk simple. I would wait at that restaurant, Heather's whatever, until Cheryl showed up. I would stay there and watch, day and night, and she'd be as glad to see me as I was to see her. I could sense this. I would just sit in my car, sleep in my car, until she made her rounds. People move. People orbit, obey the same physics as a bullet but don't hit the dirt as fast. Trajectory is all over the place, but wait long enough and they come around again. I was always chasing the past and I was sick of it. Let them come to me.

The place went dark in sections, until only a light in the kitchen serving window glowed, and then that went out as well. Some girls and a guy came out the back. One of them pointed at my car. They all got in their cars and left.

Shit. I hadn't used their bathroom. I had just decided to get out and pee behind their dumpster when a sheriff's car pulled through the parking lot, slowed and looked me over, then sped up. When he disappeared around a corner at the intersection, I started my engine and cruised down the street until I came to the Golden Horn Tavern and Grill, where I slipped into a narrow parking spot at the end of the lot, outlined in railroad ties.

The noise in the doorway was some country song I'd heard before in some stinky watering hole for enlisted types near Fort Lewis. I felt at home, gone back in time, like these were my people, like they should be glad to see me. I stood at the urinal in a cramped little can with five other big quiet dudes, my forehead against the wall to keep my balance, then went out and ordered a beer and asked the bartender if he knew—and I used only the most respectful terms—a lady, a smart, beautiful lady named Cheryl, who ran a dude ranch in the area. He looked at my face, at my eye, maybe sizing up my alcohol content, and said no.

He took my five and returned two with a wet pint, not looking at me again. I turned my stool around and scanned each table, the couples playing pool, and the handful of couples that moved around a square dance floor not much bigger than a king-size bed. Lot of nice looking girls there, big hats and tight jeans, sterling and turquoise jewelry and belt buckles, pretty pink fingernails hanging onto their men. They were all too young. Or too old. Or didn't laugh right. A short guy, maybe thirty, took the stool next to me, sleeves folded back, stars and stripes tattooed on his forearm. I tried to make eye contact, but he turned away each time I looked at him. Finally I asked, "When did you get out?"

"What?"

"I said, when did you get out?" I raised my voice a little bit and pointed at his arm.

"Out of what?" He seemed annoyed and looked away.

"Army."

"I wasn't in the Army."

"Marine Corp?" I was probably shouting then. I shout in noisy places.

"Look, I wasn't in any fuckin' army. I just happen to love my country, okay?" He took his beer and moved down the bar where he sat next to someone that seemed to know him. When I swiveled back, the bartender was staring at me, and I decided right then I didn't belong there, and I was out of control, and look how I'd pissed off this guy who loves his country and why didn't I just get the fuck out. I knew I was going to come down, then, and come down hard, realizing these were not my people, that maybe I had to have a better hat, or boots, or be from there, or show up with one of those girls, and oh how stupid I felt.

The smell of the pines hit me like ice water when I stepped into the parking lot. I staggered in the direction where I'd parked, and a primer-black pickup rumbled into the spot behind my car and three guys got out, each pitching a can in the bed as they hopped down from the seat.

"Hey," I said.

One of them walked over, face-to-face, and pushed his cap back. Indian-looking guy.

"You blocked me in."

"It's early," he said. "You don't need to leave."

"Whas'a matter Charlie?" The driver was approaching.

"He's leavin'. Says we blocked him in."

"Tell him to go fuck his horse."

Charlie was in my space, his face a bubblehead of stupidity and bad breath, some kind of provocative clown. I wanted to feel something, to hurt him, hurt him bad.

"He said to go fuck your—"

I punched him hard in the face.

Immediately, someone hit me in the side of the head. The third guy, just a blur to my left, and I back-fisted him and punched Charlie, who still stood there numbly holding his nose, three more times. Things got real kinetic after that: blow to my right kidney, a couple more, I spun and went down; tripped, pushed, maybe just too drunk. A lot of boots, my back, chest, shoulders. I covered my face, and it really wasn't that bad, I thought. Just numb enough. I grabbed a boot and twisted, someone fell, and it felt good, just what I needed; I think I was laughing, which just pissed them off more, when a boot connected with my right eye. Somebody was calling me cocksucker and a lot of other grunting. I was grunting too.

Headlights, sudden and hot as noon, enveloped the brawl. Diesel clatter shook the earth, eyes closed, dust blasting up my nostrils. The kicking stopped. Somebody got knocked down, somebody yelled "Shit," coughed, then "Shit almighty," a "Goddamnit," and three pair of boots staggered away. "Cunt," someone shouted, and coughed again.

I tried to get up and hit my head on a bumper, fell flat in the gravel, headlights passing on the street visible beneath the long, dirty under chassis of a truck. Heat felt good.

"I need to call your dad, Charlie?" a woman said.

More grumbling, unintelligible over the engine.

"Got my cell phone. He's writing a ticket over by Harvest Foods."

The grumbling receded until it was almost at the door of the tavern. Saw three blurry forms through the blood in my eye, retreating up the steps. A firm hand around my bicep helped me to my feet. It was Cheryl.

She opened the passenger door and helped me up, then took the driver's seat. Blessed quiet inside, air conditioning like snowfall. She turned on the dome light. "Jesus, you look awful." She turned my head side to side, then pressed a paper napkin above my eye. "That's going to need stitches."

"It'll be fine."

"It's bad. I'll drive you over to the ER."

I shook my head.

"Well you are definitely FUBAR."

I took the napkin and pressed it myself. "Jesus, what did you do to those guys?"

"Bear spray." She put the truck in gear and backed up, measured me with a sidelong glance. "Plenty left in the can."

She drove a couple of blocks down the highway. "Where are you staying?"

I shook my head. "I hadn't planned that far ahead."

"You're in no shape to drive." She swung into a parking lot, slowed and turned. "Looks like the Glacier is full." We swung back on the highway, headed north a half mile and she slowed. "Looks like no vacancy at the Dew Duck as well." She stopped in the parking lot and turned my head again. "That bruise over your left eye is old. You get drunk, beat up every weekend? Some people enjoy that, I'm told."

"It's a long story."

She killed the engine and rolled down the windows. "I'm listening."

"I haven't really drank since I first got out." I belched. "It's complicated." I belched again, liquid coming up in my throat. "I'd rather not."

"You going to puke?" She unlocked the doors.

"No." An Enfield hung in the rack behind the back seat. "That's a Mark III," I said, and burped.

"Good. You know your guns. You were going to tell me about this." She touched my left temple.

"There were a lot of them in Afghanistan." Eyes closed, images flickered past, silent film desert hillsides, sand in my mouth, a conversation with Garcia, but I couldn't hear him, just some emphatic gestures. He put on his glasses and turned away.

"Sit up," she said.

A police car was passing in front of the truck, turning along the driver's side. She made some reassuring gesture at the Stetsoned figure behind the wheel and it disappeared behind us. I closed my eyes again and the seat rocked gently. I might have drifted off momentarily.

"I can put you out right here or find you a place to stay." She glanced at her watch and turned toward me with a bounce of her hair. "But I've got all night to listen."

I told her about my afternoon trying to connect with "Uncle Danny," Danny connecting with my face, Danny's duct tape, Danny's little pipe, Danny's little cabin in the forest, carefully omitting the water-board segment, trying not to slur.

She sat for a long time just looking at me, unreadable; impossible to say if she thought I was a liar or delusional. She shook her head, finally.

"A lot of people in the woods like that." Her face soured. "Did he really wipe his ass with my card?"

I nodded.

She started the diesel. "So, you still don't know who your dad is."

"He's dead. About two years. I found his parents in Sunnyside last week."

"Your grandparents."

"I'm trying to get used to that idea. I'm afraid they're going to expect me to be him—and I'm not." I turned the napkin over and looked at the blood soak. "I'm some kind of warrior son of a dead psycho hero."

She put the truck in gear, rolled up onto the road. "Not much of a warrior tonight."

"Thanks." The wind through the cab was tossing her hair. "You are really, really pretty. Prettier than I remembered."

She feigned deafness for about a block before glancing over, opaque and humorless. "You are really, really drunk. Put your seatbelt on."

We drove out of the town's neon, up the highway for ten minutes or so, then into the forest, the headlights swallowed by dense thickets of trees that came at us in curves. In a few minutes we emerged into a small valley amid the mountainside's irregular black walls, a barn and ranch house a half mile further, a three-quarter moon rendering long shadows and the faintest trace of color. We slowed to a stop in front of a long, one-story structure dotted at intervals with dark windows.

"Only the end cabin occupied tonight. You'll be in number two." She helped me down and unlocked a door, turned on the light to a small room of knotty pine. I sat on the edge of the bed and she walked past, lit the bathroom and came out with a wet washcloth. She stroked around my eye.

"It's stopped bleeding. Wasn't as bad as I thought." She stepped back, regarded me critically. "Might just leave enough of a scar to remind you in the future."

I sat, feeling small, like a kid in a chair outside the principal's office.

She marched around, aloof and business-like. "Towels in the bathroom. I gave you a room with a tub in case you have trouble standing up." She rapped a small bottle on the tabletop like a snare drum. "Some Tylenol." She turned and stepped out the door. "Goodnight." A moment later she put her head in. "Whatever you do, don't go out. I let the dogs have the run of the place at night. Could tear you up pretty bad."

The tub was long and I lay in it until I fell asleep, waking when it got too cold and my head was pounding. I'd left my meds in the car and who knew what was left of that by now. The room twirled. I knelt next to the toilet and threw up. No blood, but everything else so much like Mom's Sunday mornings. "Not much of a warrior tonight," and the look Cheryl had on her face, the tone so matter-of-fact. Woman spoke truth.

I slid a window up next to the bed, opened a second in the bathroom, basking in the breeze, steady and clean. A small black digital clock glowed on the nightstand. No TV. No phone. I turned off the light and lay there for a few minutes, and remembered Garcia telling me one time that if a guy was throwing up, and his pupils were a different size, it meant head injury. *I was kicked in the head, wasn't I?* I went back in the bathroom, turned on the lights and looked at my eyes, and they were equal, and then it occurred to me that if I had a serious head injury I wouldn't be hopping around the room. Alcohol makes you stupid.

I pissed in the toilet and it was pink. Very stupid indeed. I stood there, dick in my hand, looking at the guy in the mirror, face like a bowl of crushed cherries. I'd never looked like that. That bad. Never in my whole stupid life so out of touch, out of control, out of bounds. I wiped up some of the pee that missed, some puke as well, took a couple of Tylenol and lay down again, thinking I'd never really thanked Garcia, what I might have said to him, and now he was dead; wondering just how big an asshole I had been when he retrieved me in Kamdesh.

- - -

I woke slowly as the room grew light, head still throbbing, expecting my bunk at Camp Eggers, waiting for the food carts at the psych ward, the futon at my apartment; a child's wail from a dream, bringing me fully into the day, became a small whine outside the window, white cotton curtains fluttering. Pulling on cool, stiff jeans felt good. I ran cold water in the bathroom, put my head under the faucet and drank, couldn't get enough of it. In the mirror, bruises over both biceps, an abrasion shaped like the side of a boot along my rib cage under my right arm. A thigh was turning purple. Lifting the left leg or taking a deep breath threatened to awaken all the agony of the night before.

On the step outside my door two liver spaniels lay in the sun. One just looked at me and yawned, the other sat up and sniffed my hand. I squatted and petted it. Cheryl meandered across the lawn, plaid blouse, fingers in her front jean pockets, headed my way.

"These the dogs you warned me about?"

"Cassie and Cedric. Only dogs here."

I looked around. The place was greener than I expected, the sky brilliant, the contrast of the clouds and sun over the horizon, all of it at once, too radiant, too grand. "I must have really been an ass last night, huh?"

She shrugged, touched my cheek. "I've met worse. God, I

should have given you some ice." She turned and took a few steps toward the pasture.

I followed. "How'd you end up being there, right then?"

"Paul, the bartender, called. Said there was some screwball asking around about me. I got curious."

"You go there often?"

"Darts. Tuesday afternoons. Women's league."

"Screwball, huh?"

"He might have used some other word. I sat across the street and watched you hit Charlie. What did he say to you, anyway?"

"You saw me start a fight?"

"Didn't say you started it. Figured he must have said something, that's all."

"You know him?"

"Everybody knows everybody here. Charlie Cole. Sheriff's kid."

"Great."

"Don't sweat it. You did him a favor. His dad probably arrested him anyway." She stopped at the corral fence and hung an arm over it. "I'm sorry."

"For what?"

"That you go off, fight in some awful part of the world, and come home to this. Sort of represents my town."

"It's not your fault." I took another painful deep breath and coughed. "It's weird. In the Army everybody's on the same side. Here, everybody's for themselves." I felt awkward, shirt stiff with blood and dust, jeans with a tear like a hanging tongue. Couldn't remember zipping my pants. "I should get back to my car, if there's anything left of it." I backed away. "I really appreciate this. You could have left me there. Wouldn't have blamed you if you did. I just had some funny notion in my head."

We drove back to town, me making small talk about the trees, how the drought might leave them for the beetles, trying to remember anything old Dunham said about the forest when I was a kid. I went on about the Afghans cutting down the cedars in the mountaintops without any kind of reforestation—Allah was going to do it for them—and she nodded while I tried to prove I was an ordinary person who could talk about ordinary things, be interesting. The little red poppy hung from her shift lever.

The black pickup was still parked tightly behind my car, the rest of the lot empty, *Closed* sign in the tavern window. "Looks like your friends might have got themselves arrested last night."

I climbed out of the truck and stood for a moment. "Shit."

She rolled down her window, sat there, truck idling. The parking lot was adjacent to a car wash, at the same level. I lifted one end of the railroad tie and moved it aside. She applauded.

The four beer cans still lay on the floor and I swept them under the seat, then turned my car around and came back, driver to driver next to her. I dragged the tie back in place.

She put the truck in reverse but stopped after a few feet. "You want to make any money?"

"Doing?"

"I've got a load of hay coming around noon." She glanced skyward. "Supposed to rain like stink early afternoon. Could use some help. Get it inside faster."

I followed her back out to the ranch, took an antidepressant on the way, tried to swallow it when she wasn't looking in her rearview. Her truck was battle-worn, dirty in the way work trucks could be, with a fuel tank and nozzle set across the bed just behind the cab. Diesel for farm equipment, I guessed. Was nice, made sense, to see a truck without monster tires or some stupid decal in the rear window—a giant marijuana leaf, or Calvin pissing on something. On her left lower tailgate, a black-and-white bumper sticker: *NO WATER, NO FOOD.*

- - -

Shortly before noon, Miguel arrived with a five-ton flatbed stacked with bales, a stumpy, grizzled fellow over sixty, some unspoken familiarity between them, a loyalty. They'd known each other for decades, possibly since she was a child.

"What you have to remember about horses is they keep needing fuel whether you ride them or not." She handed me a pair of hay hooks. "Ever use these?"

"In another lifetime."

Miguel had back problems and only dragged a few bales before he settled into a rambling conversation of broken English, sitting on a paint-stained chair just inside the barn door. The hay, it turned out, was grown elsewhere on the property. Miguel baled it and drove it in.

We stacked the first level on a half-dozen pallets; she paused and looked at the spaces between them.

"I figured about five inches, for air."

"Perfect," she said. "Lets the cats get in after the mice, too."

"You have cats?"

"Just barn cats." She arced her gaze across the hayloft. "Probably up there watching us, right now." She hooked another bale. "Don't like cats?"

"Cats are fine. Just allergic to them."

"I never let them in the house."

We moved another dozen bales, another layer. Get busy and pain falls into the background. "How big is this place anyway?"

She set her hooks down and gestured. "When I was a kid, we had over 2,400 acres. That house way down there sits on what used to be our spread." She pointed through the door to a mobile home about a mile away. "Now we're down to 246," she sighed. "Had good years. Bad years. Dad sold off parts piece by piece. Put me through college." She stepped into the sun, pointed, perspiration pressing her blouse to her flank. "Part of it runs up to the ridgeline. Other side is national forest land, so it's not like anyone is going to build up there."

We started stacking again. "What did you study?"

"All kinds of stuff. Boys, mostly. Got a teaching degree, then got married." She slung another bale. "Big waste of time."

"Getting married, or education?"

She looked at me, mouth askew. "We're getting kind of personal here, aren't we?"

Eight or ten bales remained when the first drops fell. We

worked speechless and fast, both retreating into the open double doors when the cloudburst hit, drops kicking up tiny puffs of hay dust until they coalesced into a thin sheen of mud, Miguel driving off slowly, windshield wipers flapping out of sync.

She set the hooks in a bale near the door, cocked her head. "What do you sell yourself for?"She looked at me from the door, cocked her head.

"I beg your pardon?"

"I never asked you. What did you expect to get paid?"

"I don't know," I said. "Just the exercise is enough." My ribs ached, my legs ached, but now it was a good hurt.

"I'll fix you dinner." She pulled her gloves off and started to the house.

"Room two still mine?"

She turned. "Till the maid kicks you out."

"How will I know what she looks like?"

She didn't turn but called back loudly, "Don't know. Haven't had one since 1996."

I showered and managed to find one clean shirt and a change of underwear. The rest of my clothes were filthy, rolled in the legs of one stiff pair of BDUs. I used to be better about this, everything in its place. I was living like a coyote.

I shaved with bar soap and a well-used throwaway razor, fascinated by the abominable face in the mirror, wondering if she *liked* looking at me, some perverse interest in violence. Some chicks liked boxers. My right eye was swelling shut.

She had a grill smoking on the porch of the big house when I came out, lifted a raw steak with a fork as I walked up.

"I don't know whether to cook this or put it on your face." She studied me empathetically. "Sorry I didn't get you any ice."

"You already apologized. I didn't deserve any anyway."

I motioned at the Volkswagen parked outside unit twelve. "Newlyweds? They never came out."

"Writer. Stays in there most of the day, sometimes he walks to the end of the pasture." She smiled. "Lot of broken pencils in his trashcan."

"Not much business for mid-August."

"Been some problems this summer. How do you like your steak?"

"Rare. Medium. Whatever's easiest." The afternoon sun lit up the valley wall like marble. "Who wouldn't want to come here?"

She uncovered a bowl of slaw and half a loaf of garlic bread, pointed at a chair.

I sat down.

"Cat attack in May. Don't know if you heard about it. Made CNN." She spooned slaw onto my plate. "Jogger, young woman, over on a forest road." She gestured at the peaks beyond the pasture. "They found pieces of her, under the brush. Family is suing the Forest Service."

"And?"

"Mid-June I got a letter from our insurance carrier, saying if the cat isn't captured or euthanized, they can't provide liability." She stood, took my plate and forked a steak onto it. "I take horses with tourists up all along those trails. That's what this place is all about."

"Panther?"

"Panthers are black. South American. Mountain lion. Cougar. Same difference."

"They ever attack somebody on a horse?"

"Probably. Not in my lifetime, though. Not when there's a dozen people on horses. They're just too timid." She tore a piece of bread loose. "Jogger was probably alone, running, cat's instinct is to chase. Late spring they can be pretty hungry."

"I can pay for my room if you like."

She laughed. "You are so kind. No, you're my guest. I appreciate any effort you make here, but I really wanted to get to know you."

"You don't know how glad I was to see you last night."

A shy silence fell for several minutes. Three horses crossed the corral. The wind picked up softly and lifted our napkins. My head wasn't hurting anymore.

"Anyway," she said, "at this rate we won't make enough this year to write off the new roof on the barn."

The barn had a gloss-red metal roof, still wet from the rain and clearly much newer than the graying cedar that supported it. "When did you put it on?"

"May."

"You can depreciate it over seven years, you know."

"You do taxes?"

"Seasonal, a couple of years after college."

"You're sure of this?"

"Was the law in 1995. I'm no expert. You'd want to check it out with your accountant."

"You're looking at her." She smiled, shook her head. "I thought you were in the Army the whole time."

"I was out for three years. Got an AA in Missoula, worked a couple of seasons at H&R Block. I'm not a CPA or anything, but I remember that."

"It's a small operation," she said. "Just twelve units. No hot tub or pool, either."

"No TV?"

"None of the rooms have one. No internet either."

"I'd think people would find that relaxing."

"I'm not sure people even know how to do that anymore." She cleared her throat. "I mean, I can get internet in the house, over my phone service, but it can be a real time waster. Stare at the screen long enough and you get numb in the head."

We sat and talked, about Colville, the Dunhams, basic training, the books I'd read, Iraq, Herzegovina, Fort Lewis. She talked about living in Okinawa, her mother who died of breast cancer, going to grade school for American kids in Italy. We talked about how odd rock music had become, everybody pissed off about something, and how everybody you heard about in the news was a victim of somebody else.

She showed me a picture of her daughter, Danielle, off in Denver at her father's for the summer.

"Heartbreaker," I said. The girl really was stunning, even at twelve—a young Victoria Principal. "I thought you said she didn't know her dad?"

"She didn't, until he surfaced again after five years."

I handed the photo back.

"He took off and went to law school." He was reliable, she said. Had remarried, a girl named Beth. Beth was okay. Danielle liked her. Wasn't Beth's fault she had no judge of character. We talked until the sun started to set.

An old man moved across the farthest limits of the drive, just beyond the barn, shuffling with two forearm crutches.

She noticed. "That's Dad."

"He doesn't stay in the house?"

"Has a cabin, other side of the barn. First house he built for my mother after he retired. When she died, he moved out there. Better view of the pasture."

The figure slowed, turned our way and raised a hand. Cheryl waved back.

"Doesn't he want to join us?" I tried to sit a little taller.

"He gives me a lot of berth. If he sees you here a second or third time, he'll get curious."

The figure shuffled beyond the corner as the last streak of sunlight faded across the field.

I explained I had some business to take care of in Spokane. She followed me to the car and watched while I stuffed my bag and tossed it in the trunk. I leaned against the door and felt awkward. She took a small step forward and touched my eyelid.

"It'll heal," I said.

"Does your mouth hurt? Your teeth?"

"No."

She leaned forward and kissed me and stepped back as quickly. "I'd like my dad to see you a second or third time."

"I'd like that too." I turned into the seat of my car, feeling clumsy, extremely un-clever in my answer. I rolled down the window and offered her the key she'd given me.

"Keep it. Doesn't fit any other door in the world except that one." She slipped another card in my hand. "Don't lose this. And stay out of bars."

I backed the Corolla around her and she never moved. As I drove down the road she waved briefly, then headed back to the house.

- - -

I was gambling. Gambling with time. It's all we ever really have, all we're ever given. You can turn time into money, or smoke, a big old house on the hill, or a whole bushel full of brass casings. You can turn it into hate. You can sell it. But when it's all gone, you got to go. I glanced at my face in the mirror. I'd have to spend at least a week or two not getting beat up.

Climbing into the mountains, up the pass where only a week ago I imagined RPGs coming out of the woods, my head was clear, full of light, as if the sun had never really set. No trucks were on the road, and maybe it was the width of the pavement, the cool smell of the wind blasting in the window, the softening of the evening into night.

In another two hours I was falling out of the mountains, out of the night, descending on Lake Coeur d'Alene. Moving lights scattered near the water's edge in a marina, one or two headed for port. I imagined being out on the water, something I'd never really done, and wondered what it might be like to sit in the stern of a boat with Cheryl, headed home, to some place anchored, warm, secure. I'd have to ask her about boats.

I took the first exit, pulled into a Tesoro station and filled up. A Dodge pickup pulling a horse trailer from Wyoming pulled in on the opposite side of the pump. In the fluorescent lights, two brown-faced horses stuck their heads out and looked at me. I remembered being on horseback once; the Dunhams took me up near the border, my legs grasping one giant, warm creature that was thinking, carrying me somewhere, knowing he could kill me, but loyal to my safety. It was intimidating and still it didn't last long enough. Cheryl could have that feeling anytime, every day, and I wanted to drive right back to her.

Don't be too eager. She said she wanted to see me again. Not exactly; she wanted her dad to see me again. A retired Air Force colonel. An officer. Not an NCO, but a real live officer—who couldn't talk. I wasn't sure how I'd handle that, leave a good impression. I wasn't sure I left a good impression with Cheryl. Might be one of those women who compares every man she meets to her daddy.

But the rest of the evening at home I couldn't stop thinking about her, imagining everything I did—opening mail, loading the washer, tearing open a frozen pizza—with her nearby; how it would be fun and novel, and all the stuff we'd talk about, and every few minutes I had to tell myself, *Don't be so fucking eager.* She probably changed the lock on that cabin minutes after I left.

The last piece of mail was a plain white envelope, return address Rural Route 7, Box 11909, Granger, WA. I set it aside and stared at it like a ticket for a journey I wasn't prepared to take. Went to bed instead, thinking about having Cheryl next to me one second, then thinking how stupid I might act, how this whole obsession to be close to someone was just absolutely the worst addiction a person could have and what a major fuckup I was about to become. I think I had bad dreams after that.

The next morning, I made a pot of coffee, sat down, opened the letter.

Dear Robert,

It was a joy to meet you, and I am sorry you felt like you needed to leave so soon. It must seem very odd to discover you are part of a family you never knew about, and not part of another.

Your arrival has added 10 years to Larry's life, he just about gave up after Ricky died and seeing you has made all the difference. Seeing you has given us closure on many questions, and opened a few new doors. It's the open doors in life that keep us moving forward.

I am sorry we lost Ricky when we did, I think the two of you have much more in common than you think. Like your father, I am sure you've been taught some hard lessons; war can be a cruel teacher. Whatever they are, embrace them, you certainly paid enough in "tuition." Something is learned from everything, and I think if your father was here now, that's what he'd say. That's my grandmotherly advice. Then go fill your life with deeds that people will remember you for.

We're both too old to drive very far out of the valley, and hope you'll come back for another visit soon.
Rita and Larry.

"Come back soon." I didn't know if I could do that; the prospect felt like donating a kidney, like I'd have to work on my facade, hide all the little cracks and crazy shit that might spill all over their life and make them regret the invitation. They didn't want to see *me*; they wanted to look at their dead boy again. Why couldn't they see that? Didn't they see they were fooling themselves? A kind of lie. I didn't want to be part of another lie. It was hard for me to connect with a past I never really had; easy for them to connect with a future that never came.

Over there, I spent years wanting a family to write to, some counterbalance to my life, and now that I was here and they were right there, a few hours away, I didn't know what to do. The Nikon rested on the kitchen table, a weight on the flattened letters. I sat and played with it, opened and closed the back, held the viewfinder to my eye. My father had looked through that same glass, at a completely different world.

10

I let a week pass, detailed the car, changed the oil, replaced filters, washed my kitchen floor, the baseboards, soaked every glass in vinegar, put odd ones in a sack by the door until I had four little ones and four pints left. Sharpened all the knives. Bought some black oxfords and polished them to mirror finish. No class A to go with them, but it didn't matter. Thought I'd feel better but didn't. Wanted to fieldstrip a rifle, any rifle, but didn't have one. Looked in the paper to see if there were any jobs working on guns but didn't find any. Bathtub got scrubbed, toilet scraped flawless, fixtures polished. Soap would spot them and I'd wipe them off again.

Sitting, turning the key over and over in my hand, I didn't know if I could trust Cheryl. *What does* she *really want?* Maybe it was the sympathy thing, but they always run out of sympathy after they know you. What's exotic and dangerous from a distance can get real ugly real close.

I hadn't trusted Jennifer. I sure as hell wasn't ready to trust Kaye, almost as soon as she opened the door. I didn't trust the scan codes in the grocery store, the few people on the bus at night who looked at their shoes, people who wouldn't look you in the eye. The headline on the magazines at the checkout, the stories about Afghanistan on the radio, all full of spin that the country was growing ever more democratic, ready to sit at the table with the grownups. Every day the Taliban murdered more people. If you couldn't hold a truth in your hand, like a bullet, it didn't exist. You couldn't trust anything.

I started to understand I probably couldn't trust my instincts, my understanding, even my memory. I drove up and down the west side of the city, all these thoughts going around and around in my head, three nights in a row. I watched the eyes of the clerk when I bought gas, the girl in the grocery, the woman behind me in line, and the guy in the BMW next to me at a light, who locked his doors when our gazes met, and then I realized—they didn't trust me either.

The following night I was headed home out of the Kmart parking lot, turning into the outside lane, taking advantage of someone turning in, when the car behind them rushed forward with a long horn blast, high beams all over my interior. I pushed down the mirror, sped up, but they stayed right on my bumper, side to side, at one point like they were going to jump the curb, pass me on the sidewalk. Apparently, I'd pulled into a void he intended to fill. Enough of this shit, I thought. I turned at a Subway a half mile farther, and they were on my ass, scraped my bumper. The driver got out, I could see him marching toward me in the side mirror, head shaved, Fu-Manchu moustache, tattoos all over his neck.

"Hey, asshole!" He kicked the side of my car. Black steel-toed boots—another welder. Closer, he kicked in the side of my rear door. I got out and stood and he stepped back, sized me up. Another guy got out of the other side, came around the front. I didn't look at his face, just side-kicked, heard him suck it up and he was out of the fight. The driver made another kick, I blocked, he caught me in the side of the face and I punched, punched again, punched fast without focus, no control, something coming apart inside of me, and I thought I might kill him. He swung and I sidestepped, backed up. I was starting to tremble; he'd come into my space, where no negotiation was possible, but I could easily fuck up the rest of my life in a heartbeat. *Gotta have control.*

He turned his head and coughed a loogie onto the upholstery, looked at me and grinned, his lip bleeding. "Jap crap car."

I watched his arms, his feet, his balance.

He pulled a sheath knife from behind with his left hand, lunged, and I caught him, pulled it across, my right elbow into the back of his, both of us against my car in one motion, my knee up in his gut so hard I wanted it to come out his back. Something cracked, he gasped, another elbow in his chest, then the right again and he went down, knee into his arm into his ribs, crushing his head against the pavement. I grabbed the knife, set the tip in his eyelid. My hand was shaking, and it cut him a little bit.

He snorted, frothed, torso twitching.

"What the fuck does it matter what I drive? What gives you the fucking right"—sweat dripped from my chin onto his face—"to run me off the road? Try to kill me?" He had a tattoo on his forearm, a dagger through a skull. "Answer me now. I'll shove this up to the hilt."

He whined, coughed and I mashed down harder. He couldn't take another breath. "What did I do to you? What's your excuse? Taliban would crucify you to a tree, you worthless fuck." I looked at the tattoo again. A smudge of ink showed at the rolled-up cuff, and I sliced the sleeve open. An anchor. *U.S.N.* "You were in the Navy?"

He glared sidelong at me, nodded. I didn't know what to say. We just glared at each other for another half minute.

A crowd had gathered and when I stood, turned, knife still in hand, they retreated clumsily. I tossed the knife on the Subway roof and they watched it rise, scattering like it might bounce back, then seemed to relax. I couldn't see the guy I'd kicked, or anybody that looked like he'd been kicked. I planted my heel on the driver's fingers and he stared at my shoe. I moved my foot and he scampered off to his big old oxidized Pontiac, dragging his left arm, a moment later smoking the tires backward, then over the curb into traffic.

I shook to pieces, like only my clothes held me together—had to stand holding the edge of my roof, looking down at his foot mark in my rear door, his snot on my seat. Someone touched my arm. I stiffened for a blow and turned. It was a black boy, about ten.

"Sir? You dropped your wallet." He held it up to me.

- - -

I found Zilker's card and gave him a call. I didn't have an appointment for his clinic, but he agreed to see me during lunch.

We sat in his office in the new wing; had that new-carpet smell, books all along the walls, mostly war, history, psychoanalysis. I walked around reading the spines while he picked through a desk drawer.

"Here." He held out a card. "Tom McEnroe. Give him a call. He's a vet, has a group that meets once a month."

There was a palm tree on the edge of the card. "Gulf War?"

"Vietnam, right up to now. You need to meet some others that are back now. Might make a friend or two."

"Therapy?"

"A kind of therapy. A chance to talk. Speak the same language."

I took the card and sat down.

He kept notes of me, probably all of his patients, in personal shorthand on a yellow legal pad. The real chart, I'd learned, was on his computer. "Excuse me." He pivoted in his chair, logged into my chart. "Any nightmares?"

"A few."

He clattered away at the keyboard. "About?"

"Same old same old. I'm in a battle. Always in the desert, just before dark. Enemy is coming and there's no fucking end to them, and they kill everybody in the platoon. All of my guys. And my rifle—" My throat tightened.

"Doesn't work. Or isn't loaded." He turned in his chair.

"How'd you know?"

"Pressure to perform flawlessly always raises equal fear of

failure. Happens to college students all the time." He looked back at the screen. "They just dream about tests they're not prepared for. How do they end, your dreams?"

"I always wake up."

"Good." Without looking over. "Today's your birthday. Happy Birthday."

"Thank you. Good that I wake up, or good that it's my birthday?"

He didn't answer but leaned back and leafed through the yellow pad, then gave me the old raised eyebrows. "Learn anything about your dad?"

I told him about the photo. I told him about the letters. I told him about Uncle Danny and he smiled and shook his head. I told him about Richard Nelson, my new grandparents. I told him about Jennifer leaving.

"So you think she split things off because you were a sniper?"

"Seemed that way."

"I think it was just your fatal flaw."

"Being a sniper?"

"No, that's not what I mean. Fatal flaw usually isn't a flaw at all. What I'm saying is she wanted out, maybe embarrassed you'd find out about her tardiness on the rent, or whatever, her poor parenting, her drug use, so she cut you loose but wanted you to think it was your fault."

"My fault." It *was* my fault. "Maybe she didn't think I'd make a good dad." Maybe I'd told her in the fog of night. A kid. Our company was crossing a field above the Pech River when we encountered about a hundred Taliban, and we dug in along a berm by an irrigation canal. I was another hundred yards or so on the left flank, without a spotter, doing overwatch, picking my targets, when I see this kid, looked like a teen, with a goat herd, practically in front of me and I fixed my eye on him, then through the Leupold, and he just seemed to be loitering, and then he opened a cell phone, and I didn't want to take him, but in a second I convinced myself he was sixteen or seventeen, and I took the shot. He sort of expanded and burst when it hit him. I could hear it, felt it in the air.

"Robert?"

"Yeah?"

"You said 'kid.'"

"Did I?" I ran forward, broke cover. Him lying there in a striped tunban, half gallon of his chest gone. "I shot a kid one time. I just remembered."

"Afghanistan?" He was hoping I wouldn't say Seattle or Portland.

"Kunar Province. I thought he was a hostile, but he was just a kid, messing with an iPod. Found it about ten feet away, blood all over it."

"And you told Jennifer about this?"

"I don't think so. Just remembered it. Unless I remembered it before."

"Robert. Things like that happen, most of the time when the enemy changes the rules of engagement."

"Where the fuck did he get an iPod?"

He looked at me and I tried to look somewhere else, and I think he wanted to hear more, but we just sat there in the silence of his new carpeting for minute after minute. Eventually I corralled my thoughts. I told him I didn't think the antidepressant did any good, that I'd almost killed a man in a parking lot after he tried to kill me, stupid fucking road rage because I happened to pull in front of him and somehow that entitled him to take my life.

"How do people get off being so fucking entitled? I felt safer in the Army. What the fuck happened while I was gone?"

"People have probably gotten a little ruder in twenty years." He glanced toward the window as if they were out there looking at us, and leaned forward, hands clasped. "Lot of young men feel they need to challenge someone to prove themselves. Same urge that made you go in the Army. Except they haven't learned what you have. They'll probably stop bothering you when you look a little older." He swiveled his chair lazily, then stopped. "Nothing is going to make what happened to you go away. What happens to us always, in some way, becomes part of us. The medications just help you change your response to emotions that come with those memories."

I told him I'd seen an old woman, who couldn't talk, who I thought was my grandmother, but who the fuck really knew for sure. I told him I didn't trust my own understanding of anything, not even the stuff I thought I saw happen—that my entire life had been flipped on its head.

"So, you understand that you have trouble *trusting*, and that it's a problem."

"I guess so, if you're wrong."

"No. This is important. The well-adjusted person, Robert, knows when they shouldn't trust a situation, when it's something they've experienced before as unreliable." He sat on the edge of his desk. "You've been so long in the land of bad surprises that your default position has become one of *constant* disbelief."

"It's kept me alive." I almost added *sir*.

"That's true, certainly when you were at war. And war taught you that life isn't worth much. Not even your own." He returned to his chair, closed his eyes and pinched the bridge of his nose. "Thus, it's a short jump to losing your self-esteem." He opened his eyes. "Do you see where this is going?"

"Like I don't think I'm really worth having?"

"Exactly."

"I was worth something in the Army. I think guys were glad I was there. I covered them. We covered each other."

"Because you *trusted* each other. But you don't think you're worth anything here, do you?"

"Doesn't feel like it. What I can do, nobody needs. If I could be like everybody else, get married, have a kid, buy a house, do all that without feeling like a phony, would do whatever it took."

He shifted in the chair. "Look. A plumber walks through a house, he looks at the fixtures. A doctor goes to a restaurant, he's sizing up the health of the people at the next table. People fall back to how they're trained, how they look at the world. You just came out of a career where you constantly looked for threat. Most of the time it's not going to be there."

I wondered what I looked like, looking for threat. Vacant. Foolish even.

"You have to trust, to make good things happen. Some people call it faith."

"And what if people lie?"

"What if they do? You get your feelings hurt. You move on. It's not like Kabul where a lie can get you killed." He scratched a few lines on his pad and looked up, pushed some new prescriptions across the desk. "Life is like a swimming pool, Robert. But you're not the lifeguard anymore. Get in the damn water. Swim."

— — —

That afternoon I drove up Sprague, over to Trent, and stopped at Big R. Growing up we had one in Colville, got my school clothes there. I don't know what to do when I go in a mall department store. A guy can't tell where the teen clothes end and serious, adult clothes start. And what is really serious, anyway? Half of it feeling like toilet paper.

I picked out four pairs of jeans, one in olive, and a half dozen shirts, two of them with little pearl snaps. I might want to watch Cheryl throw darts at the Big Horn, and it would pay to look the part. I bought some gloves, a six-pack of blue underwear, a down vest, a denim vest, and a hat.

"Your house burn down?" a red-haired bopper of a girl sniped at checkout.

"Something like that." I handed her cash and walked out with two big sacks in my hands. "It's my birthday," I called back as I pushed out the door. It was time I bought some civilian clothes, even if Cheryl wound up not wanting me. I stopped at my bank on the way home and made a withdrawal.

I packed my books, the rest of my clothes, and a loose box of kitchenware in the next hour. I stared at Jennifer's portfolio for a long time, wondered how I could get it back to her. Finally, I walked it down to the office and the manager said he'd give it to her if she ever showed up, but he doubted it. I didn't even know her last name and didn't think to ask him.

I went back and sat on the futon in my empty apartment,

placed Cheryl's card next to me and stared at my cell.

I punched in her number. It rang seven, eight, nine times, and I wondered what to say if an answering machine picked up, or if the number was disconnected—if she was gone, too.

"Harbour Ranch." She sounded out of breath.

"Hi." And it seemed incredible that she was talking to me, on the phone. "I'd like to rent cabin number two."

She hesitated. "I'm sorry. That cabin's taken."

"Really?"

"The rest of the units are quite nice."

"I'd really like to stay in cabin two."

"I'm sorry, it's not available."

"For how long?"

Trying to sound a little firmer. "Until the management says it's vacant. Why are you so set on cabin two?"

"I stayed in it once," I said. "Have really good memories."

"Well, I'm sorry. They all have the same view."

"Can't you just move them out?"

"How long do you need a room?" Exasperated. I think she was getting ready to hang up.

"Until your dad gets curious about me, I guess."

A long pause, then, cautiously, "Robert?"

"Yeah?"

"Jesus. You had me going!" She moved the phone away for a moment and laughed. "I've never heard you on the phone."

"Is the room really taken?"

"Of course not. You still have the key, don't you?"

"Hanging from my rearview mirror. I'm surprised you trusted me."

"Is there a reason I shouldn't?"

"No. I just thought people had to earn that."

"If people had to earn trust, it wouldn't be trust, would it?" She gave me a few seconds to absorb that. "How long can you—I mean, how many days do you have off?"

"I thought I might rent it for a month."

"Can you get that much time off?"

"I don't have a job." It sounded so lame. I could feel her

expression fall. "What I mean is, between my retirement and the disability from my knee, I do okay."

"I can't charge you."

"Of course you can. I'm paying rent here, I might as well pay it there. Lot quieter." I was afraid I sounded pushy, losing her. "Think about it, anyway. I could help out more. I'd try to stay out of your way."

"You don't have to do that."

"I thought I might want to go hunting."

Cheryl asked if I'd ever gone hunting. Pheasant, or ducks?

"Hunted deer when I was a kid."

"Deer season doesn't start until late October."

"I was thinking about mountain lion, actually."

"They haven't caught it yet." Her voice grew stolid. "As soon as you get in its territory, the cat is hunting you, you know. Not like deer."

"Familiar enough."

"Meaning?"

"Last seven years of my life."

"Do you miss that?"

"I think I can live without it. I know this is one thing I can do, though."

"We should talk about it," she said. "When do you think you can get here?"

"Tonight, if you like. Tomorrow afternoon. It's up to you."

"I'll make you lunch."

- - -

I left the following morning, sun rising as I crossed the Idaho state line. I didn't have a rifle, and I thought it might seem odd if I showed up with one I'd never opened or sighted in. I decided it would be best if I used one of hers. *If* there were more rifles on her ranch; but of course there were. It was a *ranch*, wasn't it? But then borrowing one of hers seemed presumptuous too.

I must have debated for an hour or more. Then I wondered what I should say, what came first, and where I should park my car. In front of cabin two seemed good enough. And I'd said I could stay a month, and she didn't say anything exactly to suggest that wasn't okay, but then maybe she didn't want to hurt my feelings, or didn't know how to say she was going to need some time to herself, and, Shit, maybe she didn't say anything because she was afraid of me, the scary murderous vet, afraid to contradict anything, and she wasn't going to be there at all, just the whole place locked up, SWAT team watching me from the barn. I invited myself. How much ruder could a guy get?

She'd kissed me, but I didn't know if that meant I should try to kiss her. The Army gave you little placards to use to communicate. Sometimes even a translator. Maybe I should just mumble Pashtu the whole time. This is really stupid, I thought. I am really, really sticking my fucking neck way too far out here.

And then I thought of Zilker. *I might get my feelings hurt.* I was thirty-six, for fuck's sake.

11

From Highway 200 I took the Los Rios Road turnoff and, for a moment, didn't recognize the next intersection. It had been dark, after all, and I was drunk and too stupid to make notes the next day.

On a hunch, I turned on East Park Road, narrow and convoluted, and then after a hundred feet or so stopped and stared at the wall of trees. I shouldn't do this, I thought. Cheryl had no idea the kind of shit I was capable of, and it would be a matter of time before I had another nightmare, or blow-up, or she figured out I really didn't have a clue how the world works now. She has friends, probably soccer moms, and how the hell will she explain me? Or maybe she could just keep me out here, hidden in the woods. Will she trust me around Danielle? She could do so much better. Maybe she just wanted a bigger barn cat. So fucking stupid; I don't belong there. Isn't that what I've spent my life doing: looking for what doesn't belong?

I'd just slapped the shifter in reverse when a rusty truck grill rolled up behind me. I watched, in the mirror, a rotund fellow with a dirty cowboy hat climb out, stand on the running board a moment, then hobble to the side of my car. I dropped my face in my hands.

"Señor Kent! I thought that was you."

Miguel.

"Something wrong with your car? You need a push maybe?"

He was so, so right. "No. I just wasn't sure this was the right road."

"Sure it is! I follow you." He turned back to his truck. I put my car back in first and rolled forward.

I stopped in front of cabin two and unloaded my bags, opened the door. The bed was made up stiff and clean. The pillow looked new. A quart canning jar sat on the table stuffed with fresh daisies and a handwritten note, *Welcome Back!* A whole bunch of worry melted away, but I wondered if I deserved the flowers. If I could live up to them.

I stowed my bag under the desk and washed my face before heading up to the house. Cheryl met me at the door, and she took my hands for a moment and gave me a quick hug. "How was your drive?"

"It keeps getting easier."

"Was it ever hard?"

"I don't know. Don't know why I said that." I *didn't* know. Maybe it was familiarity, or perhaps gradually understanding I really didn't have to watch the shoulder for IEDs. Maybe it got a whole lot easier when Miguel blocked me in.

Cheryl had set out a bowl of pretzels and two glasses of lemonade.

"While I'm thinking about it." I shoved a bank envelope across the table.

She held it at arm's length, prying the edge open with a thumbnail, and shoved it back. "I can't take that."

I shoved it across again. "Sure you can. You've got a business to keep afloat."

She started to push. I put my hand on hers.

"How about you keep it and let me know when I've exhausted the rent."

We stared at each other and she pulled the envelope slowly to her side. "I'll let you know."

It was $2,000, but she didn't open it. "Two kids on mountain bikes saw the cat last week. Swear it chased them."

"Where were they?"

"Trailer park, middle of town."

"Don't think I can go hunting in a trailer park. Definitely a PTSD kind of move."

She smiled and gestured at the ridgeline. "Anything you do has to happen up there."

We ate lunch. More steaks. Whole chest full of them, she said. Would be freezer-burnt if she didn't use them. We talked for a while and I carried the dishes inside. I started to rinse them at the kitchen sink and she stopped me.

"Later," she said, and motioned for me to follow. We walked to the end of a hall, into a darkened bedroom, the odor of musk, powder, leather in the air. Her vanity sat near the door, half in the light, the silk poppy wedged in the mirror clip. "You have a rifle?"

"Not yet." I'd run into Missoula and pick something up at a pawn shop.

She flipped on a closet light. "Take a look. See if there's anything you can use." She pushed a row of dresses out of the way and a gun rack appeared—about a dozen rifles, upright, a steel cable running the length of the trigger guards. She unlocked one end and pulled it through.

Each a beautiful work, some of them blue and rich, the stocks burled walnut, glossy as a new car. I ran my fingers along them. I picked up a little lever-action Marlin.

"You don't want that."

"But it's so cute." I ran my fingertip over the crown of the muzzle. The stock had been cut down. "Twenty-two?"

"Yeah. My gun. When I was about ten. Got a few rabbits with it."

I handed it to her reverently and she put it back. "Some of these look like they've never been shot." There were a couple of Weatherby bolt-actions, one with a price tag on the trigger guard.

"Dad bought a couple more, even after he had the stroke."

"I'd be afraid I'd scratch it up."

There was a .250 Savage 99. An M1 Garand. A lever-action .30-30 Winchester. "We took a lot of deer with that," she said. "But never further than sixty or seventy yards. You won't get that close to a cat."

Near the end, another bolt gun, battered, the stock one dense shade of walnut, flat and greased. It looked familiar. "Winchester 70?"

"Very good."

"We had some at Fort Benning." I picked it up, a 3-9x Leica scope already clamped on tight, the objective about three inches across.

"Dad's bear gun."

"Looks like he dropped it once or twice."

"Might have. He didn't take family along when he was after a bear."

I squinted at the receiver and held it up to the light: *.338 Winchester Magnum.* "Will he mind?"

"I think that's the one he'd want you to use."

- - -

There were eighteen tarnished cartridges left in a desk drawer, in an oily, blue-and-yellow cardboard box from an earlier era. I drove into town the following morning and bought two more boxes, some ear plugs, and a package of five targets. In the afternoon, I paced off 400 yards, then drove a couple of hay bales down to the point I'd chosen, fixed a target in place while Cheryl coaxed the horses into the barn. I stood in the far side of a corral, barrel resting on a sack of feed slung over the top rail, an ancient pair of AO hearing protectors clamped over my head. In an hour I had a group of about three inches after dialing the crosshair as low as it could go. Whatever bear Cheryl's father shot with that gun had been pretty damn close. He stepped out of his cabin briefly and watched but didn't join us. I guess he wasn't curious enough yet.

- - -

It rained that evening and the following day. I spent the afternoon mucking stalls for the workout, until Cheryl discovered me there and said I was going to make Miguel feel inadequate. I showered and we ate, then sat on her porch for a while in two rockers.

She leaned back and hovered there a second. "You're not a bad-looking man, with your face in one piece."

"Thanks."

"What was it like? Over there."

I looked at her, maybe a little too critically.

She steeled herself. "I'm serious. I really want to know."

"Afghanistan?" I didn't know where to start. "That's where I was last."

"Okay. Start there."

"Iraq you've seen on TV." I hesitated. "Kind of like West Texas. Where I was, anyway. But Afghanistan . . . is like no place on earth I've ever been. The central highlands lead right up into the Himalayas." I told her how it could look like New Zealand or like the badlands, and sandstorms could rock your Humvee, flip over a port-o-san, tear tent stakes out of the ground, and about the dirt everywhere, even between your teeth for days after. "But it was beautiful. Sometimes. Like a stained-glass window." And I stopped.

She looked at me almost like Zilker would look at me. "And sometimes it wasn't."

"It wasn't like at the end of the day you could savor it, soak it all up." I pointed at her pasture. "Usually I was just stupid with exhaustion. I remember, when the whole thing started, somebody compared the Taliban to the IRA. The IRA, they said, was trying to bomb their way to the peace table. The Taliban just wanted to blow up the table. The people themselves were stuck in the middle." The sun dropped out of the valley. "The war was just bigger than them," I told her. "Any of them. Their world was their village, or their valley, and they grew to hate whoever was bringing the most recent misery to their valley."

The people were friendly, sometimes a deceit but mostly genuine—a kind of hospitality unknown in the Western world,

I explained. But they had grown to hate the Russians, then the Taliban. After a while, we too wore out our welcome.

I tried to describe what it felt like, looking out the back of a CH-47, the serrated peaks of the Hindu Kush, snow-crusted and unmarked by roads or towers, rivers bright with the sky's image, the cold clarity of the air; even as I got older it left me wide-eyed. In Iraq I spent most of my time thinking about myself, trying not to get shot, just to see Colville again. And I told her about being married for a while, and how damned trivial everything Julia and her parents were caught up in seemed; life was a joke for them, and eventually I couldn't wait to get back in. After that, I started paying attention—to the people we'd come, ostensibly, to save, and more so to the young men I was expected to keep alive.

"Getting rank was a little bit like having a family," I said. "In the beginning we were all brothers, but by the end I loved them like they were my kids."

"What'd they call you? Your kids."

"Sarg." I smiled. "Or Chief. When they knew I could hear 'em, anyway."

"You miss that?"

"You see them arrive, full of bravado, grab-ass and badass, and after a few weeks they're quieter. Professional, even." I wasn't sure how to put it into words. "Nothing makes a kid grow up faster than war. Then a couple of them die, usually fast, right in front of you. So, no. Don't miss it."

"Sarg," she repeated. "Should I call you—"

"Anything but Sarg, okay? Robert. Or Robby would be fine."

She seemed put off for a second, I could sense it in the darkness, but she took my hands across the table. "Then Robert it shall be." There was strength in her hands. She let go and lit a citronella candle, and her face warmed with color.

"Why aren't you married?"

"I was. Got divorced. I told you that." She squirmed a bit and got that same expression she had the night she picked me up drunk.

"And nobody else was interested? I'm not buying it."

"I'm not going to ask you about all of your—"

"No, no, that's not what I mean. I just wondered what you're doing with me. Why hasn't some guy at the Big Horn brought you flowers?"

"Lot of guys don't want a kid. Especially some other guy's kid." She relaxed, shook her head in disbelief and smiled, took my hands again. "You're the first one who's given me a flower in a long, long time." She reflected a moment, pushed her hair back. "There's a guy I went to college with. Lives over in Bozeman. Terry. Computer engineer, makes good money. He calls me every once in a while."

"And?"

"He's a nice guy, really. But still wears his cap backwards. Sits on his sofa, plays games on his big TV. Keeps telling me I should get on Facebook. But the real problem . . ." She stared into the dark, then turned back to the candlelight. "He's afraid of horses."

We were quiet for a while, me drifting on memories of horses, of the Dunhams, Mr. Dunham taking my knight at the dining room table. "You play chess?"

"No," she said. "You?"

"When I was a kid. Not much since." I started a game once in Camp Tillman but couldn't remember finishing it.

"My dad and brother used to play. I'd like to learn."

"It's a deal."

We were quiet again. From across the grass two wolfish silhouettes meandered up the steps and over to our feet where they lay down.

"Why Harbour Ranch? Nowhere near a harbor."

"Dad said he wanted someplace we'd all feel safe, like we could always come back here, no matter what might happen to us."

"A safe harbor."

"Yeah. His first name choice was Fort Redding. Mom wouldn't have any of it."

"Fort?"

"Yeah. He said it was *defendable*." She gestured into the evening. "Those trees, on the other side of the pasture? He used to point to them and tell me that was our *perimeter*."

I looked around the expansive darkness. "It *is* defendable," I started to say, but down the valley somewhere there was a pop and I stopped breathing. She heard me stop breathing.

A few seconds passed. "Hey. Are you alright?" She started to stand up, lean across the table.

"There was a guy. Big guy. A lieutenant named Dunbar, commanded my platoon my second tour, for a month or so. Came with a badass story you could smell; guys said he'd been dirty in Iraq, one of those guys that steals from the locals, does their daughters, in the name of looking for guns."

"My God. And nobody does any—"

"Nobody wants to snitch because they're scared." I gathered my thoughts, wanted to tell her and yet didn't want to risk anything, risk her trust that I wasn't really fucked up. "So," I said, "one night he's sitting there with one of the squads, rambling on what he knows about war or what his daddy knew, and he liked to sit higher when he was talking, and he was tall anyway, and suddenly he stops mid-sentence. Mid-word, really. I look up and it seems like he's shaking his face, but it's really his face coming off, and his forehead turned into a mist."

"Oh God. Oh no, please, no."

"I'm sorry," I said. I reached out, took both her hands, found her gaze.

"Why did you tell me that? I wasn't expecting to—"

"I'm sorry. It's just that a second or so after, after Dunbar got hit, we heard the shot. A little shot way off in the distance, like that one. I just wanted you to know why I get nervous sometimes. You need to know about me."

"They were probably just shooting at a coyote." She wiped her cheeks and I realized that she had started to cry, but she managed a little smile. "I promise, that won't happen to you here." She rubbed my forearms briefly before getting up to clear the table. She looked back. "Maybe Dunbar deserved it. I know you don't."

- - -

Deserved it. Didn't deserve it. I don't know. If you start divvying up the deaths like that, you go nuts way faster. People just want bad shit to make sense, and that helps them, and I was not going to argue with her. She was better off not knowing.

I fell asleep that night wishing I had more time to apologize for telling such a god-awful story, but mostly thinking how good her hands felt in mine, trying to relive that touch and the dim relief of her expression across the table, imagining us nose-to-nose in that little bed. Defendable perimeter, Cheryl at the center. Giddy, warm, feeling like I was fifteen all over again. Horses I could deal with, but I was still afraid of a lot of things. She asked me about my *kids*. I pictured her, round and full, even with her little streaks of gray, and the image glowed, and I think I fell asleep with that in my head. Garcia would have approved.

--- --- ---

It rained intermittently the following day, clouding over by the time I came out, a cool wind coming off the hills, pouring for twenty minutes or so, and clearing with a rainbow, a series of them across the floor of the valley by the day's end. Amazing how densely green a pasture could look after a rain.

We sat that evening on the porch swing, a swing long enough we might have lain in it, and talked—about being little kids once, and what we'd thought we were going to do, and year by year how people could turn into something else. She had always, since girlhood, wanted a ranch in the mountains.

"You ever tell your dad that?" I plumped a cushion next to me and she slid closer.

"You mean, like he made all this happen just because his little girl wanted it?" She shook her head. "More like he planted the idea in me." She rocked the swing gently with the tip of her toe and then stopped it, foot on the rail. "He might have done that for my brother."

I turned, looked her in the eyes. "Where is your brother? You never told me."

"I *had* a brother. He's dead."

"I'm sorry."

"I was ten. I cried a lot when it happened, but I really miss him more now that I'm older." We both leaned back again; she pressed into me and spoke into the night air gathering beyond the porch. "He was twenty. Stationed in Germany."

"Army?"

"You kidding? Air Force. Anyway, bought a motorcycle, got drunk on leave, got himself killed." She turned on the cushion to face me and put her arms around my neck. "So you see, I'm not going to stay close to people who drink too much. Understood?"

"Understood."

She pulled my arm around her shoulder and wove her fingers between mine. "So, what's the worst thing you ever did?"

"That's getting very, very personal."

"Really," she giggled. "It's one of those questions you're supposed to ask people when you're—"

"When you're what?"

I felt her blush. "Getting to know them."

"I'd have to think about it. Done a lot of awful stuff, really. You first."

She crossed her arms. "Hmmm," she said. Then looked at her feet and shook her head. "There was this girl, in high school. In Italy. Her father got her an Alfa Romero. Was real snooty about it. Picked up *my* boyfriend at the time and drove him up in the hills, never found out what they did." She looked at me, lips pursed. "Took me and a friend into Latisana, left us 'cause she'd met some guy and didn't want us in the car. Used to skip classes and go to Lignano Beach, lie around in her bikini. We followed her one time. Cut her distributor wire."

"*Cut it?*"

"Yeah, cut it. So she couldn't just pop it back on."

"She get towed home?"

"Worse. She'd apparently been flirting with these older guys, Italians. When she went to her car, they followed. Hassled her. *Polizia* showed up, chased 'em away, then arrested her because she didn't have any ID."

"A high school kid?"

"Italians were big on terrorism, even back then. They called the Carabinieri. Carabinieri called the base, Air Force MPs had to come get her." Cheryl laughed, then composed herself. "Didn't get home till the next day. Rest of the year, a Jeep dropped her off at school, picked her up. Completely screwed her social life." She scooted to the far end of the swing, her back against the arm, and faced me. "Now you."

"Like I said."

"Come on." She poked with her socked toe.

"I—"

And Kamdesh came clear to me, like opening the roof of a house and spotting a secret room. Trying to reach a shooter, climbing a ladder. Guy at the window shouldering an RPG. I raise my rifle but it's empty, action locked open. He turns, RPG discharges, exhaust burning my face, bounces around the room and blows down a wall. We struggle on the floor, me trying to break his neck when I slit his throat with my Gerber. I can smell him, he stinks, and I just keep sawing, his blood pouring, pumping out of his carotids all over my hand, wiggling the blade between bone until it tears free. I'm holding the head, taunting the enemy, sunlight and bullets coming at my face, mouthing off about virgins or something.

"You just flinched. Don't make anything up, now." She was still there, smiling.

I shook my head. *How do you tell a woman you did such a thing?* I have no idea why I did it myself. You scare people with shit like that, because in their safe little notion of how the world should be, they can't picture *themselves* ever doing such a thing.

"There was this girl," I started. "In high school."

"No fair. You can't use the same story."

"Ninth grade, actually. Mom was still alive. We used to sneak out."

"You and who?"

"Brandon. Best friend. Had a car when he was sixteen. Anyway, we drove to this girl's house one night, about 3 a.m. Picked the window I thought would be hers. We lit a cigarette."

"You smoked?"

"Brandon did. Don't think either of us inhaled. But we took a string of firecrackers, put the fuse through a cigarette, left it burning on the windowsill."

"No way to impress girls."

"Turned out, it wasn't her room."

"Oh my God."

"Was her dad's. And he'd been in Vietnam. Really went berserk, I guess."

"She ever talk to you again?"

"She didn't talk much to me to begin with. But ruined my chances for good." And in that moment I felt worse, worse than I'd ever realized—how cruel it must sound. "I think I know what it was like for her dad. Haven't thought about that night for ages."

We sat quietly.

"So, you speak Italian?" I asked.

She perked up. "Do you?"

"No. Just some Pashtu. Few phrases of Urdu."

Eyes narrowed and scanning the heavens, Cheryl enunciated slowly, "*Penso che—mi piacerebbe avere un figlio con te.*"

"What did you just say?"

She just smiled, shook her head. "Just something all Italian girls say, sooner or later."

"You're not going to tell me."

She scooted over and pulled my arm back around her. "Maybe someday I'll show you."

12

The third morning began overcast but blew over by ten, and I set out wearing my remaining pair of Danners and full BDUs, knowing it would take the better part of the day to reach the tundra where I'd have the best hunting. I spent the night prior in my cabin reading a book titled *Cat Attacks*, none of it especially sympathetic to cougars. They especially like to eat kids, grab them by the head. I mused for a while on making a fake kid decoy—drag it on a wire or something, few ounces of C-4 in the skull—a joke only the guys in the platoon would find funny. Cougars are sneaky bastards. Eat the liver out of your cocker spaniel while it's still alive. Kill your house cat and eat it on your lawn. I learned a new word: *Crepuscular*—active at dusk and dawn. They creep around at night, too, but prefer to hunt in low light. They can spot your carotids.

I reasoned that if I took the higher route, with less cover and less likelihood of being ambushed from behind, I'd have the tactical advantage of high ground, a better vantage point to search from, and the remaining daylight when the brush was falling into shadow.

In addition to the rifle, I loaded a three-liter Camelbak

and two sixteen-ounce bottles of water, six salted nut rolls, a blanket, and two sandwiches Cheryl handed me before I left. I didn't plan on eating much; this was a mission. I'd learned about the enemy, *Felis concolor*, reconnoitered the terrain. *Get in, do the job, get out.*

I slipped the Tokarev in my pocket before I left, not so much for protection but out of fear she'd run across it while cleaning the cabin, this crude Russian pistol, and perceive it as a low-life factor. She would go through the things I left behind, I was sure of it. Who wouldn't?

I started on a horse trail leading out of the pasture, beginning as tire ruts but narrowing to about five feet. I could walk uphill all day, but I couldn't run with any kind of load at all, so triggering something to chase me wasn't going to be a problem. Found myself briefly looking for Russian mines in the grass, PMN-2s, dusty little hockey pucks left over from the Russian invasion. After thirty minutes the trail grew abruptly steeper, still recognizable between the rocks, marked periodically with balls of dry horse manure. The sun grew hot in the afternoon. I had a round in the chamber and the safety on; not the responsible way to navigate uneven ground, but I trusted the rifle and my own discipline to keep the muzzle low.

Heading west first, walking into the sun, I waited for my vision to recover in the shade from one cluster of trees to the next, knowing that the ridge ended after a couple miles of steady rise, leaping one fissure after another, every fifty yards or so, thinking it might be best to search that section of the hilltop first, like you'd clear a house of many rooms, but not fully appreciating that each fissure housed another plane of travel, crisscrossing below me, and the ledges twenty or thirty feet down—so many hidden paths an enemy could backtrack and, without a whole platoon, it was impossible to recon with any credibility.

I knew this starting out, and the knowledge kept coming back, but I was too comfortable, falling into how I'd been trained. I drank little of my water. The sun splintered over the horizon and then it was gone, and I was falling into shadows quickly and hadn't really established a perimeter, any sort of safe zone.

I dragged one fallen tree trunk near another to form a *V*, still thinking I needed ballistic cover, set my pack at the apex of the *V*, built a small fire near my feet in a shallow in the rock and stretched out under the blanket.

A crow screeched like a klaxon, bobbing on my foot, picking at my boot laces. I shook my foot and he spread his wings, rose a few inches, and settled to pick again. I smelled cold ashes. Morning. I sat up halfway and froze. Ten yards from my feet, motionless, unblinking, sat the cat. Even seated it was nearly four feet tall. Imperturbable curiosity, or patience. Maybe it wasn't hungry. I glanced at the rifle and remembered clearing the chamber before I dozed off. I took a breath and the cat did the same, a quick motion of its ribs, an inhalation of me, testing the air. I rolled, grabbed the rifle and screamed as I stood, launching forward, locked in the notion that the cat would fear the muzzle of a gun. The cat sprang back and, before I could work the bolt, had vanished down a ravine. I ran a few steps, limbs half asleep, boot strings untied.

I went back to my useless little camp of two logs and a fire long turned ash, chambered a round and set the safety. I tied my boots. I shivered and peed on the other side of the log, as if I were going to stay there. I sat down and realized I hadn't brought any coffee.

Setting out as the sun rose, I ran the lower ledges, coming to the top every hundred feet or so, rolling my heels and stalking in a way I hadn't since the days with Mr. Dunham, hunting deer, crossing from one side to the other, determined to clear that end of the ridge, looking down into the trees and trying to lessen the notion, the very likely notion, that the cat could shadow me under the mantle of the forest. They didn't like midday, I'd read. They weren't supposed to, anyway. Should have found out what time the girl was attacked or what time she had set out that day, then look for some shadowy area, a shallow cave, with a sleeping cat. But dwell too long on what you hope to find and you'll get blindsided.

By midday I crossed the first short plateau I'd ascended the day before, and worked my way northwest, trying the same tactic, but the ridge's width expanded to a half mile and it simply took too long to cross the top; the whole operation started to feel senseless.

My legs were tiring and my back hurt from sleeping on stone. When I thought I might fall asleep again, I shouldered the pack and went on. Sometime that afternoon, a song got in my head, a memory of Brits singing in a pub in Bosnia, getting drunk. "*I get knocked down, but I get up again, you are never gonna keep me down . . .*" It just went on and on in my head, might have even sung it out loud but couldn't remember all the words.

It would require a platoon, maybe an entire company, to do this mission justice.

I drank one of the water bottles while I sat, pack under my arm, wondering what kind of impact it might have on Cheryl if I didn't come back, slipped over an edge, or got eaten; how unfair to put that burden on her and how fucking arrogant to announce I was going to kill a cat, just march on up here by myself, when every operation I'd been on in the last eight years was really a choreographed effort of several hundred people. What the fuck was I thinking? That I could find the cat, paint him with a laser and radio some Apache pilot the position?

The sun got hotter and the song played on in my head.

▪ ▪ ▪

Just after sunset I spotted motion on the crest of a smooth rock face about 600 yards away, a dun speck bobbing, swaying in the fading light. I sat and raised the rifle, sling triangle-tight against my elbow, elbow on knee, peered through the scope and eased off the safety. It was a cat, maybe *the* cat, walking leisurely, tail swinging side to side, narrow hips left to right, across the vertical axis. Too narrow. I couldn't take a shot; a fifty-fifty chance I'd miss. I gently rotated the zoom, all the way up to 9x, but it was still too narrow. The wind was in my face and the cat hadn't smelled me.

It turned sideways and stood for a moment, holding something in its mouth, something it had killed. I let out some of my breath, held, set the crosshairs on the shoulder and squeezed. The recoil rocked me, but a second later the cat went airborne, the object in its mouth flung free, and it was gone. I worked the bolt, chambered another round and stood. My ears rang; I hadn't thought to put on the protectors. No sign of the cat, the flash of my muzzle still a blue image central in my vision. I moved quickly, crouched instinctively for return fire, and searched the horizon for some irregularity. I crossed one large crag, leapt a small fissure, crossed another, each mass of stone pitched, leaning into the surface, ankles turned to stay upright, deaf to the sound of my own footsteps. The sky grew impermeable, colors fading, night falling fast. In another hundred feet stood a clump of pines, dwarfed and twisted horizontal by the wind. I side-stepped between them, needles across my eyes. Granite crumbled beneath my weight, and I very nearly went over a ledge, fifty or sixty feet down. I backed up, seized a pine branch, clicked on my flashlight and looked around. About fifteen feet from a drop-off on two sides, I'd hiked to the corner of a plateau and would need to backtrack an unknown distance to the east to get across—if I could cross at all. It was just too dark without night vision. And it occurred to me: *The cat has night vision.*

The pines rose in a tangle against the darkening sky, one of them splitting its branches like an upturned hand to the heavens. I climbed up into the palm of that hand, swung my pack under my head, and watched the stars appear slowly through the stratosphere.

I ate a salted nut roll and drank but tried to leave at least half of the Camelbak for the sunrise. It wouldn't take long to find the cat's body, just had to be able to see where I was going. I pulled the last sandwich out of my pocket and ate half, and thought of Cheryl preparing it the previous morning, her touch when she gave it to me.

The wind died, and after many changes of position I fell asleep. Shortly after midnight I opened my eyes and the sky had clouded over, the moon obscured by a high ceiling, my hand barely visible. The rocks below, where they dropped off, moved. Something dark grew larger, rising over the edge of the stone, serpentine and silent. I reached for the rifle and it was gone, left by the base of the tree maybe. *How stupid was that?* And then it moved into a shaft of light, the moon returned, and it was the cat, beneath my tree, carrying something in its mouth. It looked up and dropped the object, which hit the ground dully and rolled. Marsden's head. The cat leapt up the trunk.

I gasped and jolted, wide awake, rifle barrel cold and wet in my hands. I sat shivering, gulping air until my pulse slowed. Thousands of stars filled the sky, limpid crystals silent, low, almost within reach, the Big Dipper high in the west. Beneath it, at the horizon, a smudge of yellow light that I imagined was Harbour Ranch. The damp had penetrated every seam of my clothing, my skin, every bone. I drew the blanket tighter and repositioned myself, looked down at the ground for Marsden's head, but of course it wasn't there.

Marsden was a funny-looking kid, expression always a bit surprised, more so as he lay dying. We teased him because he read the Koran out loud to us sometimes, trying to figure it out. We'd tell him he was only interested in the seventy-two virgins, 'cause he sure as hell wasn't gettin' any in this life, with a face like his. But he wasn't an ugly guy, really. We just liked to keep the joke going. I've decided it isn't the features that make a person shine but what lights up inside them. Just about everybody has a little light if you know them well enough.

I spent the spring of 2006 in the Korangal Valley, my third tour, stop-lossed and ready to get out, living with the constant awareness that if I got scared, really scared, the enemy would see it and I would die there. Most Taliban weren't known for their sharpshooting, but they had damn good snipers there, trained in Iran, with Dragunovs and PSLs, and it seemed logical that one day my head would burst, hit by a Russian round from a half mile away. Or, maybe like some stupid tragedy, hit my spine, and I'd spend the rest of my shitty life in a wheelchair, somebody else wiping my ass and cleaning the sores. I'd just made E-8, master sergeant. Certainly couldn't look scared to my platoon. And I was scared most of the time, except at night, when the quiet descended and the sky was cold and clear, very much like Montana.

The Big Dipper was down near the horizon in the south, barely ever climbed above the tallest peaks, like a flag over a distant home, where you really wanted to be. I pulled night security a lot, just to bask in that little dream. Most of the platoon was new to me those last months and I didn't try to get close to them, just said what had to be said, avoided eye contact, told myself I was being a better sergeant. The truth was, I didn't feel like I belonged there anymore.

Now I *was* home, and the Dipper overhead seemed just as remote. The night does strange things with time; minutes awake drag by like hours, fall asleep for a moment and hours pass. I wasn't sure I belonged here either.

Did my fear of an empty chamber kill Marsden? I was so focused on myself those last few weeks. My duty was to my brothers, my kids, all of them fifteen or sixteen years younger than me except Garcia. I didn't deserve—had no right—to be part of a family. No fucking right. Hillbilly boy of a white trash woman who drank herself to death.

I sweated in my coat, pulled the Velcro apart, loosened a button and then another.

The wind blew steadily, soft through the pines, a gentle *hush* that any other night might have set me on point because it could cover the stray sound of an approach, a whisper or clatter of a magazine against stone, but on this night it felt good, and I dried off, eventually buttoning up.

- - -

When I awoke again the sky was lightening, a breeze picking up, fresh pine, bright and clear. Dew dribbled along the stock and barrel of the Winchester and I dried it off. The pack felt wet, as if it had rained.

I looked down at the ground, thinking I'd see cat prints. The valley was full of light, cool blue sky and wind, birds singing somewhere below. I imagined telling Zilker, like he was sitting next to me, what happened that last day at Kamdesh, and knew I could get it right. I took a drink, dug through the pack, found another nut roll, a thousand other memories returning.

Blanket rolled and repacked, I ate the last half of a damp sandwich and got underway. The previous day's climb had beaten up my knee more than I realized, and I hobbled the first hundred feet or so, until I reached a crevasse about fifteen feet deep and too wide to jump. It only got wider to the east, so I lowered myself in half steps, then began the gritty climb up the opposite side, realizing I was vulnerable as hell should the cat still be afoot. My hands slipped, my gloves sliced on the edges, my legs just didn't lift me like they used to, even without body armor and the gear I carried in the field. I slid back to the bottom and stood there panting, considered pulling my pack off and flinging it over the top, but it only weighed eight or nine pounds.

It didn't make sense that I had become so weak in two years. It didn't make sense that a couple of drunk twenty-somethings could beat me up. Rescued by a woman, a civilian, for fuck's sake. Almost killed by an old junky. Time in the hospital, time in rehab, must have taken a toll. I could climb like a spider a few years ago. I hadn't taken my medication for two nights or that morning, and waves of heat came over me—the tremble, the flinch at the unexpected snap of a twig, the tinge of nausea that came before losing all coordination, swept up in a rain of adrenaline. Possibly useful if a guy wants to run like a gazelle, or fight, but a disaster in the bottom of the hole. No hydrocodone either, but eventually that kind of pain just becomes a part of you—a mean part.

I threw everything but the rifle over the top, slung the Winchester across my back and jumped, scrambling, spreading my legs to both sides of the crevasse initially, a frantic series of grabs that pulled me, after a minute of terror, up to the level stone, a fistful of scrub in one hand. I crawled a few yards and sat up, panting, holding my knee. White granite spread before me, more or less flat. An irregularity, fur rustling in the breeze, lay forty yards or so distant, near a fine splatter of blood. A dead rabbit. The cat was close. High clouds moved across the sun in an overcast.

Another hundred yards and the stone rolled off, a smooth contour not visible from the distance, streaks of dried blood running down the polished surface, dropping into a hole about eight feet below. The surface of the hole rolled off again, and below that, less than six feet, a narrow trail. A dry horse turd. The wind picked up, fluttered through my shirt. The sweat evaporated from my neck.

I stared at the turd for a long time, imagined Cheryl leading a string of ponies with kids, their parents. Clueless city folk. The valley clouded over. *What if it rains?* I didn't bring a poncho. Thinking of everything but dropping into that hole. Some CS maybe. A grenade would be perfect. Alas, no grenade. Somebody to watch my six, another to cover the exit, but I was alone, and I really didn't want to do what I said I was going to do: face an enemy that couldn't talk or listen, had no sympathy or remorse, wouldn't reason. What tugged at my gut was not unlike my last nights in Korangal.

If the cat was there and still a threat, running away wasn't an option. I was going into its fucking house and it had every right in the world to kill me. I locked a round in the chamber, laid my face against the rock, arms spread, and slid in.

A narrow gap opened, tight at chest level, wider closer to my knees. Crouched, I saw three spotted kits, fifteen or twenty pounds, retreating from my smell, probably, amid a pile of pine needles, cat crap, shreds of skin and bones, gathered into a nest of sorts. No sign of the big girl, but so much of the den was out of my line of sight I felt certain she rested just around the corner. I stood, holding the rifle in my right hand at arm's length as I entered, finger gently on the trigger.

Halfway through the gap, the cat dropped to my left from some point above with a hushed thump and stood looking at me. The space was too narrow to turn, bring the rifle to bear. The cat bared its teeth, my left hand slipped around the Tokarev, thumbed the hammer, the cat leapt and I fired a double-tap blindly. Knocked into the stone, head snapped against the granite, I hit the ground, squirming backward into the den, the gun's muzzle on point, cat on my chest, my legs. The cat didn't move, the reverberation in that small space—cat's cry, pistol shots—a continuous deafening pressure. One of the shots had surely gone stray; the other took a corner of its head off.

The slide was locked back on the pistol. I hadn't fired two shots. I'd fired nine.

I stood. Something nudged my foot. One of the kits worked between my legs and ran to the body, sniffing, puzzled, searching for a nipple. A ragged hole fired from the side pierced the belly, some dried blood. The rifle shot had been low and toward the hindquarters. The blood loss probably weakened her. Two other kits cowered against the stone, looking at me. They'd starve. Or maybe they'd grow up and kill a jogger or two. What age do they start catching little mice and what age was I looking at? I just didn't know. One of the kits hissed at me, another played with a spent brass from the Tokarev, rolling it around with its paw. Strips of nylon fabric were visible among the detritus. I dropped the magazine from the pistol, slammed another into the butt and racked the action. A few raindrops fell, streaking the wall.

There had been a house, really just a hut, in a little hamlet north of Kandahar. Late afternoon. We were tired. I covered from the end of the street. Garcia cleared one house, walked out, just said, "Kids." Got about thirty feet away and a skinny boy, maybe nine or ten, pops him in the back. Single round from an AK. Two smaller kids next to him, all in the doorway. Garcia gasped, screwed his face in a picture of pain, went down. Three or four of our guys, one of them on the 249, instinctively returned fire, five or ten seconds. All three of the kids were cut to pieces, bloody fragments blown back into the shadow like a sack of offal thrown across the stone floor. Garcia started crawling and it turned out his SAPI plate had taken the round, knocked him off his feet, probably broke a couple of ribs. We all felt like shit.

Neighbor lady, maybe their mom, screaming like a demon, women in black burkas swarming out of everywhere, indignant hatred thick as smoke converging on the patrol, everybody with rifles leveled, backing around Garcia, who sat up and cried. He felt the worst, he explained later after retelling everybody half the night, because he'd cleared the house. It was *his fault*, he reasoned; he hadn't found the gun. We all thought, *WTF, parents are shits for not teaching them the rules of the game, as if it is some kind of fucking game.* The AK was empty. Kid only had one cartridge.

I stood there looking at those three kittens, Tokarev still in my hand.

13

I pushed the cat with my legs initially, then dragged it by the tail to the edge of the den, shoved it onto the trail below and stood looking at it while I caught my breath. The cloud ceiling had fallen almost to eye level. I was close to the Continental Divide, 10,000 feet, I decided, attributing my fatigue to that. I considered cutting off the head of the cat, bringing it back as proof, but it was a bloody mess, and I'd made a little vow to myself about collecting heads earlier that day. Forest department could see it from a helicopter, or ride up that trail, wherever it came from, and retrieve it. A stair-step of rock rose from the den on the far side and I went up, retrieved the rest of my gear and came down, jumping over the cat and wincing downhill. Looking back, the cat could have taken any rider that went past right off their horse, like a customer in a sushi bar.

I finished the last of my water and slowly traversed the hillside, every joint on my left side feeling like thumbtacks inside, flinching before my foot hit the ground. I sat a few times and my leg would pop when it straightened it out. That was new. I'd make sure I was on a horse if I ever had to come up here again. Raindrops spotted my sleeves, my face, fog rolling up the valley.

After an hour or so, great boulders of moss-speckled basalt peppered the landscape. I'd probably descended a couple of miles or more north of the point where I went up and was on somebody else's property. Each step chaffed, a stab, a little pull like pliers in the skin of my calf. On a level rock I sat and pulled my pant leg up to the knee. Something metallic and brilliant sparkled at the apex of the swelling, now pressed tightly beneath a pale tent of dead skin. Brushing across it stung like a hornet.

I studied it another minute or so, finally placed a thumb on either side and squeezed, a rush of tears following, a spiral of steel rising out of the skin like a worm, an inch long; a few drops of pus and thin blood followed. I rolled the fragment between my fingers. Part of the RPG in Kamdesh.

"That's one you missed, Lori." The pain faded after a few minutes. The rain fell, heavy drops across the broken skin until the red washed away.

By three, the hillside leveled off and a few minutes later I was out of the trees and crossing the meadow, haze shrouding the hill, a steady wind out of the west, and nothing hurting enough to make a difference. It struck me then that I was just taking it in, and I'd come into many valleys probably just as beautiful but hadn't really been seeing them, because I was always looking for what didn't belong; but in that moment it was clear that everything I saw there belonged there—even me. Confidence in the earth, the air that made waves of the grass, it was all there long before me, millennia, and it would continue in some marvelous balance I could only intrude upon briefly, but I was a part of it for now.

Garcia wasn't anymore. I had killed a big cat but only a small part of the continuum, myself even smaller. It was a violation the earth could absorb—infinitesimal, really, balanced against the many men I'd killed, each of them thinking they were the center of a universe when in fact none of us are the center of anything.

Patrols could last two or three weeks, but now two nights seemed like enough. I opened the bolt of the rifle with my palm over the receiver and thumbed the cartridges out, checked the chamber and closed it again. Bolt handle, receiver, my skin all about the same, wet cold.

- - -

When I got within a mile of the corral she was riding toward me across the meadow, out of the mist, pony at a trot, hair crushed sheepishly beneath a broad canvas Akubra, rain dripping from the brim, hips fluid with the rise and fall of the horse as if they were one being. She saw me and sped up to a canter, hoof-steps palpable in the earth. A feeling of relief rolls over you when you're going to be extracted from a mission and you hear the chopper blades or one of your APCs comes rumbling around a corner. I think I felt that with those hoof beats. She circled behind, slipped off the saddle and dropped next to me a moment later, reins in her hands.

"That was a neat trick."

"This is Melody. She's a neat horse."

I glanced over and I swear that horse nodded.

"I was worried to death about you." She gave my arm a terse little shake. "Afraid I was going to find little pieces of you up there."

"I thought about taking my cell phone, but there's no service for me here."

"Kept looking for you last night. Hoped you'd come late, bang on the door."

I wasn't sure how to read her. "Told you I was packing to spend the night. Maybe two."

She stiffened, tugged my wrist to a standstill. "Please, don't ever do anything like that again. Let the Forest Service take care of it. I was a fool to go along."

And she went on, but all I could feel was my arm around hers while I tried to figure out how to apologize. She pulled a water bottle out of the saddlebag and I drank half of it.

"You catch it?"

"Killed it." Water dripped out of my mouth. "Very dead."

"How big?"

"I tried to drag it. Maybe 200 pounds."

"That's a really big cat. Where?"

I stopped and we turned. "This side of the ridge." I tried to point out an outcrop of rock but couldn't be certain through the clouds. "About two hours walk."

"Might be on our property. Forest Service can go find it." She hugged me, kissed me. After a few minutes Melody grew impatient, the barn in sight, and tugged us to go.

— — —

I lay in the tub and soaked. Between the wet afternoon, the cold night in the tree and bits of dream that still lingered, no amount of hot water could thaw the chill. There were times in the field I went unbathed for three or four weeks, just a little packet of wet wipes for crotch and ass; now I felt like I could never get clean enough. I ran the hot water longer, turned it on and off with my toe until the level neared the overflow. I decided I'd write to Garcia's wife. That would be a start.

It was getting dark when I walked up to the house, the cloud cover breaking up, a hint of sunset on the mountain peaks. Cheryl had made soup and a loaf of bread, the air heavy with oregano and baked yeast. Her father rose from a beat-up wingback when I came in, extended his left hand. He nodded, then looked through the bottom of his glasses at my open shirt collar and carefully lifted out my dog tags, turned them in his hand like he was making sure they were real, dropped them back in my shirt.

"Rangh?"

"I beg your pardon?"

"Rangh." He turned his shoulder to me, slashed an invisible chevron on his bicep.

"Oh. Master sergeant. E-8."

He seemed pleased with that, slapped me on the shoulder and went back to his chair.

"Dad was a colonel, weren't you Dad?" She helped him to his feet again, to the table. "But he was Air Force, so you don't have to take orders from him."

He looked at her woodenly, pulled his arm away and sat at the head of an old oak clawfoot. He seemed embarrassed about speaking and preferred to point at things, face crumpled in thought. As we finished, he set his spoon down, wiped his mouth, shook his wrist at me and mumbled, a question on his face.

I glanced at Cheryl.

"I think he asked if you did any good over there."

I really didn't know. "Been asking myself that since I got back. Seemed like it at the time, but they seem to be tearing it down faster that we were able to put it back together. You can't give people something before they really want it." I wanted to tell him the only democracy they'd ever understand would be a separate little government in every single valley. "They have a humility," I said, "with an incredibly ignorant kind of arrogance."

Both of them stopped eating, in a somber reassessment of what I'd said, as if I'd been mean-spirited.

"Every Taliban we captured, really any Afghan we talked to, had this notion that the Taliban had brought about the collapse of the entire Soviet Union."

"You can't be serious." Cheryl picked up her glass and some tension in the room relaxed.

"Dead serious. Soviets left in '89, whole Eastern Bloc fell apart after that. They watched the wall go down on TV and thought they did it, that God was on their side."

Her father shook his head and I think he understood my point.

"Now they think they can whip anyone. God is on their side. Hard to convince a Jihadist otherwise."

"Do you think he's on *our* side?"

"I'm not sure he has a dog in this fight. Whole business is a house of cards."

Her father cocked his head like he might say something else, then picked up his spoon and went back to his soup. He seemed congenial but left after he was done, bidding us both goodnight with a wave. We watched him hobble down the steps, disappear into the gathering darkness.

"Your father's had a stroke. My mother had a stroke, granddad too. Probably just a matter of time, I'll have a stroke."

"When you do, at least I'll already know the language. You going to go see them again, your grandparents?"

"I don't know. I think they're expecting somebody else."

"You should get to know them better. Give them a chance. They're probably good people."

"I don't know what we'd talk about."

"They're your clan. Your real family. Besides, I think I'd like to meet them."

"Really?"

She stood, shot me a coy half smile, and went into the kitchen.

When she returned she took the wrist of my shirt. "And what are these?"

I'd worn the shirt with pearl snaps. "Thought I might go into the Golden Horn, sometime. When you're throwing darts."

"Very fancy. I'm going to have to start thinking about you in a whole new way." She paused. "Robert."

I helped her clean the table until she shooed me onto the porch. She came out a few minutes later, drying her hands. We sat in the swing. A thin glow of pink remained on the highest peaks to the east, reflecting the sun that had settled behind us thirty minutes before, the sky birthing the first glitter of stars. I wondered if there was some way somebody could take a picture of that. She settled in next to me. The rain had left the valley cool. Both of us were tired, and we sensed we could be quiet with one another and it was okay. About thirty minutes passed.

"You handy with a chainsaw?"

"Used one a few times. We had them in the Army, part of the rescue gear."

"Thought we might go up in the hills, get some firewood tomorrow. Cold winter coming, I'm told." She rested her head against my chest. "Get any sleep at all last night?"

"I'm supposed to take medication at night," I said. "I forgot to take it along."

She was stroking my hand but grew still.

"I have dreams sometimes. Most of the time. If I don't."

"Things you remember?"

"Things that never happened, mostly, but might have, or might still." I rubbed her shoulder. "They don't mean anything. Sure can mess up a night, though."

I told her about first sighting the cat, that first shot, my night beneath the stars, sleeping in the tree. I didn't tell her about waking up with the cat staring at me. It seemed too pathetic. But I told her about the dream. And, finally, I told her about Marsden, and how the whole world that was Michael Marsden, his kids, his grandkids, all the good he might have done, wasn't going to happen and it was my goddamned fault.

She pulled my arm around her shoulders and drew herself close. "Do you believe in God?"

The swing came to a stop. I don't know if it was her or me who put their foot down.

"Afghans, Taliban, believed that if they hit one of us it was because Allah willed it. He controlled the bullet. If I shot and missed I just shot again, adjusted a little for windage. Usually hit them on the second try."

"Your point?"

"I don't really know how a god intervenes in wartime."

"Maybe he brought you home." She nudged the deck softly and the swing moved.

"That song," I said. "God is watching us . . ."

"From a distance."

"Yeah. A distance. Ninety million miles maybe. They say Saddam had a vat of acid to dispose of bodies. Sometimes he threw people in still alive. I think we make our own heaven or hell right here." How much cynicism she'd tolerate I didn't know. "I don't think any deity is coming back for us, ever. Any of us. And the sooner everybody gets their dim little minds wrapped around that idea, the sooner the world will be safe again."

She drew a deep sigh and I wondered if I'd trashed my chances.

"I'm sorry," I said. "I guess I'm still mad about some things."

I told her that I would try to be a good man but couldn't

promise that I'd always be right, that every shot I took in life would always hit its mark. I couldn't promise that I could protect her, or anybody for that matter.

"How old were you when you started? Eighteen?" She pulled my other hand across, holding both of them in hers. "And now you're thirty-five?"

"Just turned thirty-six."

"I just turned thirty-five. Maybe we can protect each other. But you're going to have to forgive yourself." She stood, moved behind me, and buried her fingers deep into my shoulders, thumbs probing every weary thread of muscle, every taxed ligament. I loosened slowly and she rested her chin on my shoulder.

"They're not out there, you know."

"Who?"

"The enemy. They're far around the world, in someone else's lifetime now." She kissed me long on the cheek, slipping slowly to my neck. "I need to shower. Go get your medicine, then come to bed soon. I'll leave the hall light on for you." A moment later the screen door closed.

I sat looking into the night, level and treeless until it melded into the base of the mountains. Her old man was right; it was defendable, a good perimeter. I sat a while longer, a light breeze from the mountainside rising, while the moon broke over the pines on the foothills, its reach crossing the black pasture, a shimmering trestle of green and yellow that ended just feet from the porch in the gravel drive. I thought about the cubs, high up in their cave, huddled upon one another for warmth, starving for a mother that would not return.

That same moon was high above Colville, the Dunhams' house, the high school dark and empty up the hill, the trailer park in Addy, the gravel roads we cruised as kids in cars, thinking we would all live forever. That same moon above the hop fields and alfalfa surrounding the house where once my father lived, and eventually died, and then the house was ash as well.

That same moon shone down upon mothers of so many young Afghans, who wept in the night, who would never see their sons marry, young men infused with the notion that some righteous, angry god was on their side, had been on their father's side and their father's father's side. All of them believing they were descended from some great line of warriors, death but a brief step to interminable ecstasy, but destined to be dust, fed on by the fungus in the soil of the Kunar Valley, and 10,000 places like it. How close I had come to joining them.

It was inevitable. They would be here eventually, or someone like them, fists and rifles and banners in the air, clumsy hatred on their lips. I would need to rest, stay fit, and practice, and always, always be ready for that time.

CREDITS

I never went to war. I never received an invitation. My lottery number was just too high in 1972. I have—perhaps an unintended penance—spent ten years or so caring for veterans of a half dozen wars, in VA hospitals, listening to their stories. Collectively, I don't think there are a finer cohort of individuals on this planet. This work of fiction, of course, does not reflect the life experience of a particular soldier, but might easily relate to *any* soldier.

Many, many books were helpful to me in my research. The few that repeatedly come to mind are listed here, and I highly recommend each of them for a better understanding of those who have served in combat and lived to tell their stories.

War and Redemption: Treatment and Recovery in Combat-related PTSD. Larry Dewey, Ashgate Publishing Company, 2004

Cat Attacks, by Jo Deurbrouk and Dean Miller, Sasquatch Books, 2001

The Forever War, by Dexter Filkins, Vintage press, 2008.

And Then I Cried: Stories of a Mortuary NCO, by Justin Jordan, Tactical 16 Books, 2012.

WAR, by Sebastian Junger, Twelve Books, 2011.

Every Man in this Village is a Liar, by Megan Stack, First Anchor Books, 2010.

Black Flag Journals, by Dennis John Woods, Koehler Books, 2016

Afghan: Insurgent Tactic, Techniques, and Procedures, Vol II. Published by Marine Corp Intelligence Activity group, 2009.

"Driving Related Coping Thoughts in Post 9/11 Combat Veterans," Maria T. Schultheis, et al, Federal Practitioner, December 2017.

The following works of music are quoted under the doctrine of Fair Use:

Chumbawamba, I get knocked Down, 1997

Andre Benjamin, Hey Ya! 2003.

And many thanks to my wife, Sheryl, the multitude of veterans, workshop participants, colleagues, cold readers and mentors who had the time and patience to read this manuscript and help form it into the book it is today. To you all, I am eternally grateful.

ALSO BY RAYMOND HUTSON

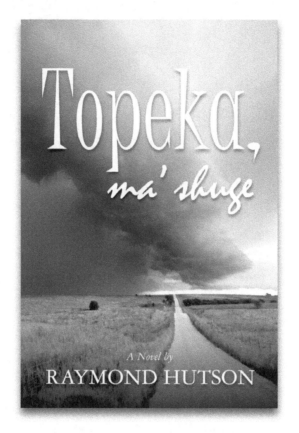

A DARK COMING OF AGE STORY.

"Though set before the events of 9/11, and never once uttering the word 'terrorism,' the book draws heavily on real-world happenings in 1989, from the influence of the ayatollah to the first World Trade Center bombings, fostering a timely paranoia that addresses, if only superficially, both Islamophobia and fundamentalist Muslims' fear of Western influences. An impressive debut that . . . establishes a constant and ingeniously engrossing sense of discomfort."

—Kirkus review